LT Kincaid
Anderson, Mar
Forbidden fir
Naiad Press,
1996.

D1409199

Forbidden Fires

Nell Kincaid

Thorndike Press • Chivers Press
Waterville, Maine USA Bath, England

This Large Print edition is published by Thorndike Press, USA and by Chivers Press, England.

Published in 2002 in the U.S. by arrangement with Maureen Moran Agency.

Published in 2002 in the U.K. by arrangement with the author.

U.S. Softcover 0-7862-4346-5 (Paperback Series)
U.K. Hardcover 0-7540-4981-7 (Chivers Large Print)
U.K. Softcover 0-7540-4982-5 (Camden Large Print)

The text of this Large Print edition is unabridged.
Other aspects of the book may vary from the original edition.

Set in 16 pt. Plantin by Myrna S. Raven.

Printed in the United States on permanent paper.

British Library Cataloguing-in-Publication Data available

Library of Congress Cataloging-in-Publication Data

Kincaid, Nell.
    Forbidden fires / Nell Kincaid.
        p. cm.
    ISBN 0-7862-4346-5 (lg. print : sc : alk. paper)
    1. Large type books. 2. Women journalists — Fiction.
3. New York (State) — Fiction. 4. Politicians — Fiction.
I. Title.
PS3561.I42533 F67 2002
813'.6—dc21   2002020265

Forbidden Fires

Chapter One

Amanda Ellis looked across the desk at Carlotta Somers, WKM's assignments editor. With her violet silk dress, pale pink nail polish, and neatly pulled back blond hair, Carlotta looked more as if she were ready to attend an exclusive gallery opening than to give Amanda her first assignment as the television station's newest reporter.

Carlotta had been studying a clipboard on the desk in front of her since Amanda had first sat down in the office, and now, when she finally looked up at Amanda, her gray eyes were hostile. "I might as well tell you," she drawled, reaching for a cigarette, "that I was against your being hired, Amanda. Frankly, I just don't see enough experience in your background, enough hard-news reporting." She paused to light her cigarette, and Amanda tried to quell her natural impulse to defend herself; her boss, Stan Daniels, had warned her that the decision to hire her hadn't been unanimous, and she knew her best bet was to ride out the storm smoothly, proving herself through her actions and her performance on the job.

Carlotta exhaled a cloud of smoke and continued: "You spent six years in Albany, Amanda, yet you did only five stories covering the state government, I see from your résumé. Obviously you were at the mercy of your assignments editor to a certain extent" — she smiled — "as you are at mine. But I wonder why he or she never saw fit to develop you in the hard-news/political area — or in any other area besides human interest."

Amanda took a deep breath and leaned forward in her chair, brushing her thick auburn hair back from her face. "We had an exceptionally good ten-year veteran on the political beat, Carlotta, and I wasn't about to try to horn in on his territory. But in any event I was much more interested in human interest at the time, and my editor respected my wishes. I was good, so there was no reason for him not to."

"Then why the switch?" Carlotta demanded. "For women these days there are still more opportunities in 'soft' news than in hard." She shrugged. "You've chosen a very competitive area. WKM is sixth in a field of six, but this is still New York. You might have a rough time of it."

Amanda shrugged. "I'm sure WKM

8

won't stay in last place for long. Stan's new approach is much too good for last place. We just need time to catch on." She paused, collecting herself for what she feared might develop into an argument. "But to answer your question about my interest in politics," she began carefully, "I assume that we're discussing this simply because you're interested." Carlotta looked at her blankly. "What I mean, Carlotta, is that I've *already* been hired as a hard-news reporter, concentrating on politics. You do know that — ?"

Carlotta sighed. "Yes, well, never mind." She looked at her watch. "I have another appointment, Amanda, so we'd better get on with it." She looked down at her clipboard and then back at Amanda. "Have you ever heard of the Harrison Commission, Amanda?"

Amanda thought and then shook her head. "No, I haven't. I —"

"Well, at least you're honest," Carlotta cut in. "All right, there's a press conference down at City Hall today at three o'clock. They're publicly announcing the formation of the Harrison Commission, and you're going to cover the press conference."

"Which is about — ?"

Carlotta ground out her cigarette in an ashtray before replying, and then she spoke slowly and with exaggerated patience, as if she were speaking to a child. "They're looking into the way permits are issued in this city — health permits, fire permits, building permits, that sort of thing." She sighed. "I realize it doesn't have the zing of the political scandals you'd like to cover, Amanda, but we all have to start somewhere, don't we?"

Amanda's heart sank. Carlotta had sounded as if she were going to give Amanda an interesting story — against her better judgment, of course — and she had just assigned her to what sounded like the most boring press conference on earth. But Amanda wasn't going to give Carlotta the satisfaction of knowing how disappointed she felt. She leaned forward and looked Carlotta straight in the eye. "Obviously you don't think it's an important story, Carlotta, I'm sure nobody does. But if there's an angle to it — and you know as well as I do that you can find an angle to anything — I'll find it. I think you'll be surprised." She stood up. "I won't keep you any longer. I assume I can get all the specifics from your secretary?"

"No, I have the information right here," Carlotta said, handing Amanda a press release with some hastily scrawled-in notes on it. "Now Stan wants to see your prelim copy

10

by noon, and you'll have to leave with one of the mini-cam crews by two o'clock at the latest. You'll take crew three."

"Fine," Amanda said, turning to go.

"Oh, and one more thing," Carlotta called out.

Amanda turned at the door. "Yes?"

Carlotta reached for another cigarette and lit it before speaking. "Stan asked me to pass this along to you: When you're at the conference, be sure to position yourself at the front." Her nostrils flared. "I understand that the head of the commission, Eric Harrison, is only too happy to cooperate with the press when the press is — female."

Amanda paled. "Eric Harrison? The lawyer Eric Harrison?"

Carlotta looked surprised. "Yes. Why? Do you know him?"

Amanda spoke as calmly as she could. "Yes," she said quietly. "At least I *did* know him, years ago. My ex-husband went to law school with him, and I worked at his law firm years ago, as a paralegal."

Carlotta raised an eyebrow. "Well, then. Perhaps you'll get a good story after all. Obviously I don't need to tell you the story can use a little help; so do play up your past connection with Harrison for all it's worth."

11

She frowned. "So your husband is a lawyer, Amanda?"

Amanda shook her head. "*Ex*-husband. And no, he's in real estate now. Law is just a convenient extra, I guess," she said vaguely, and left the office in a daze, wondering how, in the space of a few minutes, her first assignment at WKM had turned into one of the most difficult of her entire career.

A few minutes later, as she sat in front of the mirror in the ladies' room, Amanda tried to pull her thoughts about Eric Harrison together; she certainly wouldn't be able to function very well at the press conference if she reacted to the sight of him as she had reacted to his name in Carlotta's office. She imagined how he'd probably look at the conference: a tall, powerfully built man with an easy smile and a deep, resonant voice, taking command in his sure but steady way, answering questions as he always did — wittily, confidently, and just as he wanted, without giving away any more information than he chose to.

His brown eyes, too, gave away just what he wanted; she remembered how those eyes had told her husband nothing that last day, when Greg had picked her up at work and spoken with Eric. Eric had acted as if there hadn't been anything special between himself and Amanda, never suggesting that the reason she had left was that they both knew it was too dangerous for her to stay, that they could never stay apart. And she remembered other times — hundreds of times — when those deep brown eyes had hypnotized her, nearly drawing her into his arms and his life in a way they both knew was impossible. It was at those times his eyes said what neither he nor she wanted to hear: that he was married, and she was married, and what each one was thinking could remain only a fantasy — forever.

She remembered their first — and last — kiss, when she had been unable to resist those eyes any longer. Eric and Amanda had been alone in his Rockefeller Center office, on her last day; she was standing by the window, he by his desk. And suddenly she was aware of his gaze, on her breasts, her mouth, her eyes, and he said, "Come here," softly yet in a way she couldn't say no to. As if in a dream she walked to him, her eyes never leaving his, and he pulled her to him, his lean, hard body suddenly pressing against her so that she arched against him, wanting to feel the length of him along the curves of her body. Their lips met gently at first, teasingly, temptingly, and then hungrily, as he held her with greater force, tasting and exploring and flooding her body with a desire he was never to satisfy.

Even now she remembered the feel of his body against hers, the strength of his desire, which had made her want to throw everything away to be his. It was a physical memory that had haunted her through long, lonely nights, that had made her body ache from the need he had created in her, that only he could satisfy.

In the years since she had last seen Eric, and in the years since her divorce, she had thought of him often — during the nights when sensuous memories were reawakened, during the days when she'd see someone whose eyes or hair or lips would remind her of him — and she wondered what it would be like to see him again, how he might have changed. She also often wondered how important she had been to him; after all, they had known each other for only six months. Yet during that time, for her he had been a bright moon in an otherwise dark sky, the only source of joy in the long bleak days and nights preceding her divorce. She had never known, though, how he had truly felt about her, aside from his obvious physical attraction to her. It had all been so long ago — seven years, she was surprised to realize;

perhaps he would remember her only as someone who had worked at his office, if he remembered her at all. But no, that couldn't be true; he was the one who said they were getting too close, he was the one who first saw the danger in their situation, who had asked her, finally, to make a sacrifice so that they could each try to save their marriages. No, he wouldn't have forgotten her.

Amanda looked into the mirror, trying to gauge how much she had changed over the years. She had been twenty-two then, fresh out of college, blushing nine seconds out of ten and as naive as could be. She had changed drastically, she realized, physically as well as emotionally. She was much thinner, her once-voluptuous figure now slim, and the auburn hair once worn in short curls was now in a glossy shoulder-length pageboy. But her eyes hadn't changed a bit; in an otherwise plain face, with a small mouth and a slightly upturned nose, her eyes were a spectacular blue, and tilted up at the corners with long, thick lashes and clear, opalescent whites.

Amanda looked away from the mirror and down at her hands, which she had clenched without even realizing it. Would Eric notice she no longer wore a wedding ring? She closed her eyes, imagining the scene: Eric on the stage of the press auditorium, fielding questions from the audience, at one moment serious and the next joking easily. And then Amanda would call out a question, and Eric would turn to her, and their eyes would meet. . . .

She shook her head. No, it wouldn't happen that way; it wouldn't be anything like that, and she was wrong even to fantasize about it. Eric was married, even if she no longer was, and he felt as she did about the sanctity of the marriage vow. What had she even been thinking? No, she'd simply be friendly and polite, and leave it at that. And whatever desires she had to make things different, whatever feelings she had about the matter, well, she'd just keep them to herself.

Amanda soon forgot her concerns over seeing Eric as the hour of the press conference drew near. Until today she had followed the other WKM correspondents around the city, learning how they set up their reports differently than she had up in Albany. It was much more complicated in New York City, Amanda had discovered, primarily because of the crowds and the traffic tie-ups that were always created by the sight of a television crew anywhere in the city. Despite rumors to the contrary,

New Yorkers were as curious about what was going on in their streets as were residents of the sleepiest town in the country. Pacing the report, too, was a difficulty Amanda's fellow reporters had warned her about. Stan Daniels, the news director, liked to check the background information that reporters planned to put into their broadcasts before the reports were actually filmed; an important aspect of WKM's approach to news was that it was important for everyone to understand the broadcasts, even if they hadn't listened to the news in months. But it was often difficult if not impossible, Amanda's colleagues had warned, to include any background information at all in the time one actually had on the air. There were simply too many stories to fit into the program, and too little time in which to broadcast them, and thus each story had to be much shorter than its reporter wanted it to be.

By the time Amanda hopped into the front seat of the mini-cam van, she was as nervous as she had been her first day on the air in Albany. Stan had simply handed the preliminary script back to her and said, "You'll probably have to improvise anyway," turning to the phone in what was apparently his usual manner of dismissal, and now that she was looking at her notes, she wished she had had more time to delve into the background of the Harrison Commission. She would have had more time, she realized, if she hadn't spent so much time thinking about Eric!

Suddenly the van lurched into a gigantic pothole, and Amanda's notes scattered to the floor.

"Sorry about that, Miss Ellis," the driver said. "I forgot to warn you this might be kind of a rough ride."

Amanda gathered up her notes and smiled at Al, a huge burly man who looked as if he could have lifted the entire van out of the pothole with his bare hands if he had wanted to. "That's okay," she said, "there are potholes in Albany just as big as the one we just went through, and some days I felt as if we had driven through every single one in the city. The truck our station had was about seven years old, and seven years for a mini-cam truck that's used about eighteen hours a day is a lot."

Al gave a low whistle. "You're telling me. What kind of a station was it? Some kind of cable network?"

"No, just a little station. Same as WKM, really, in that it was the lowest-rated for local news in the whole city. But we were really beginning to pull up in the ratings when I left to come here." She winked at Al. "And I think WKM has a good chance of making it, too, Al. I really do."

Al shrugged. "I don't know, Miss Ellis —"

"Amanda, please."

Al smiled and nodded. "Amanda, then. I just don't know. People around here are slow to change, you know what I mean? They like what they're used to — what they call 'reporters' joking around on camera, that kind of stuff. If it was up to me, Amanda, I'd put some of that stuff in your reports." He shrugged. "Course, if they'd wanted me to step in as director, I guess they would have hired me, huh?"

Amanda laughed. "I guess so. But you *are* their top cameraman, so who knows?" She looked away from Al to the street signs. Fourteenth and Second Avenue. That meant they were getting close to City Hall. "I guess we'll be there in a few minutes, then," she said hopefully.

Al gave a philosophical shrug. "Probably, but you can never tell. We've got quite a ways to go yet and the traffic down here can be murder. You never know."

Amanda looked at her watch. "Well, it's two thirty already, Al, and the press conference is at three. Are we going to be able to get set up in time?"

He shrugged again. "Sure hope so."

Amanda suddenly wished she had a cigarette; she had quit six months ago, but now she desperately wanted one. But she wouldn't give in; she'd relax and simply assume they'd arrive at the conference on time, and concentrate on doing as well as she could. She'd have to try to forget it was her first broadcast at her new job, a job she'd been wishing for and working toward for years. What was the serenity prayer her mother had had on the kitchen wall for so many years? "God grant me the power to change what I can, to accept those things I cannot change." Well, she'd try. She'd do whatever she had to do to make her first report interesting, honest, and on the mark. And as for Eric — well, as the prayer said, she'd have to accept what she couldn't change.

The corridor outside the press room at City Hall was anything but the mob scene Amanda had anticipated. Al and the crew were carrying the Porta-Pak cameras and mikes through a virtually empty hallway, and Amanda followed them into the press room with ease. Thanks to Al's deft driving skills, their timing had been perfect: the conference was due to begin in fifteen minutes. Then why was the press room virtually deserted?

Amanda looked around at the other people in the room. In the front row of folding chairs two men who were apparently print journalists, without crews or cameras or mikes, sat talking with each other in low voices, uninterested in who else was there. A pretty young woman from one of the all-news radio stations stood across the room from Amanda, with a sound crew behind her, and a man from the other all-news radio station stood near the stage. And that was the entire audience. None of the networks had bothered to send anyone, and Amanda guessed that the afternoon paper didn't think the conference was important enough to cover, either.

She shook her head, wondering how she was going to find an "angle" to something that was being given virtually no press coverage. Carlotta had obviously known it was an unimportant event.

Al lumbered back from the aisle in front of the stage, where he had set up the man with the mini-cam. The sound crew was securing wires along the aisle. "Setup okay, Amanda?"

"Yes, Al, that looks fine." She checked her

watch: five minutes to go. "Let's go ahead with the sound and light checks, Al. I want a few minutes to look over my copy."

"Sure thing," Al said, lumbering back.

The checks went smoothly, and Amanda was pleased she had long ago learned to be impervious to the withering gazes of the print journalists present. It was no different here from in Albany; the newspapermen acted as if she were making a cosmetics commercial on the site of whatever story was breaking, as if she were just playing. In fact, this had been true to some extent in Albany, but she knew — as they would soon know, as well — that the reports shown on WKM rivaled the best print stories in the city.

After finishing the checks, Amanda sat down in one of the folding chairs a few rows back from the front. She had to study her notes, and she also wanted to make a decision as to whether she'd mention the fact that neither of the other TV stations had sent a reporter. Unless she handled it properly, it would simply sound as if the story were unimportant, a complete nonevent. But if it turned out that the conference was the beginning of an exciting investigation, the fact that WKM-TV had been there at its inception was a fact Amanda wanted the public to know. Well, she'd decide when she heard more.

She went over to where Al and the crew stood in front of the stage and confirmed the shots she wanted, and then took a new seat in the front row, microphone in hand.

And then, just as Amanda decided to make a few changes in the script, Eric appeared.

He wore no jacket — only a white shirt that fit across his broad shoulders and powerful chest, and dark linen slacks that hung perfectly on his narrow hips and long, lean legs. He exuded all the confident masculinity and easy grace of the years before, but seemed even more confident, as if he had successfully faced dozens of challenges with ease in the years since Amanda had seen him.

He strode across the platform, smiling ironically at the nearly empty room. "I can see that none of your editors think this story is front-page material," he said, laughing as he arranged his papers on the podium, "but trust me. The time will come when this auditorium will be jam-packed." He smiled. "And the six of you will have been with me from the beginning."

He looked from the reporters at the back of the room to those at the front, and then at

Amanda. His eyes betrayed a flicker of recognition and curiosity, and then left Amanda's gaze quickly, as if avoiding an as yet undivined danger.

"Of course," he went on, "this is only the beginning, and as you all know, sometimes the beginning of something isn't nearly as exciting as the end can be." He looked at Amanda again, and once again without a sign of recognition — but certainly one of interest. "What we have here may be one of the most dangerous trends to have hit the city in years — a trend that has endangered the life of virtually every citizen of and visitor to New York many, many times over. What we have here is a trend born of greed, born of a total disregard for human life, a total disregard for the laws of this country." Once again he surveyed the reporters, but this time skipped Amanda entirely. "Now as you all know, the public establishments of this city — restaurants, bars, hotels, theaters, buildings such as this one — are licensed by dozens of city agencies. They're inspected — supposedly, at any rate — for everything from fire hazards to health hazards to questionable business practices. So that you, as citizens, can be reasonably sure, as you enjoy your dinner or movie or play or hotel room, that you're not endangering your life by doing so." He paused, the only sound in the room now coming from the whir of WKM's cameras. "Now, the work we've done so far is just preliminary, but it unfortunately indicates that massive corruption — massive — exists in virtually every one of our so-called 'safety' departments. Our job now is to probe further, for as long as it takes — until we discover we've been wrong, or that we're right and it's time to clean up the problem and prosecute."

A hand shot up from the front row, from one of the newspapermen Amanda had seen earlier. "Mr. Harrison, just what has the investigation shown so far? You haven't given us names, dates, anything other than your own personal assertions."

Eric answered without hesitation, and Amanda smiled inwardly at his confidence. "The conference isn't over, Hawkins," Eric said. "But let me say, since you asked, that today I will *not* be releasing any names. The investigation must proceed without jeopardy or interference from any corner — including the media." He smiled. "But I assure you we're working with more than my own 'personal assertions.' " He looked around the room, again avoiding Amanda's eyes. "Any more questions before I go on?"

The pretty young woman from the all-news radio station raised a delicate, pale hand.

Eric looked at her and nodded, his eyes sparkling.

"Mr. Harrison," the young woman began. "I wonder if you can tell me at this point whether you have any plans for a political career. There's been talk of your being nominated as one of the Democratic candidates for senator now that you're so visible to the public."

Eric just barely suppressed a smile. "I have no specific plans, Miss Hayes. But perhaps if you have some ideas we can discuss them further — at another time."

Amanda felt an unexpected twinge of jealousy as she watched Eric look the young woman over with obvious appreciation. With a surge of adrenaline, she raised her hand, without even knowing what she was going to say. But he'd notice her, dammit, if it was the last thing she did!

Amanda felt the camera and Eric's eyes shift to her as she prepared to speak, and her throat muscles contracted as her mind went blank.

And then Eric's whole expression changed, as his eyes widened, and then softened, and he realized, at last, who she was.

Amanda was dimly aware that seconds

26

were passing as she and Eric stared at each other. But their gaze was locked, as she looked into eyes that hadn't changed in seven years, eyes that were looking at her with unmasked pleasure.

Amanda looked away, concentrating on a point on the stage behind Eric, and spoke, afraid that Eric might make some sort of embarrassing remark; he was obviously completely uninhibited about speaking of personal things in front of a camera.

"You're a criminal lawyer, Mr. Harrison," Amanda began, rather more forcefully than she had meant; her words had come out like an accusation. She continued more gently. "Does your appointment as chief counsel of the commission mean that if and when charges are filed, they'll be criminal rather than civil?"

He smiled broadly and completely inappropriately, obviously as a "hello" rather than in response to her question. Amanda's heart pounded in anticipation of what could be an embarrassing moment on her broadcast. What if he made some comment about how far she had come in the years since they had last seen each other, or how different she looked?

But he just winked and said, "An interesting question from a reporter who seems to be new to this city. Well, it depends," he began, and Amanda inappropriately but irresistibly listened with only half an ear as Eric answered in detail. She couldn't help feeling somewhat disappointed that he was able to deliver a virtual speech in response to her question, while she could hardly concentrate on what he was saying. Well, what did she expect? And what had happened to her vow not to turn the meeting into an emotional one?

As soon as Eric finished answering Amanda's question, another of the newspaper reporters' hands went up. "Mr. Harrison, let's get back to politics for a minute. You seem to be taking the kind of firm stand that's often a prelude to political nomination. Do you honestly have no plans to seek public office?"

"None whatsoever," he said flatly. "Next question."

"Now wait a minute," the reporter yelled out. "What's with the sudden brevity?"

Eric raised an eyebrow. "Are you serious?"

"I just find it odd," the reporter said. "There's usually a long speech attached to a denial like that."

Eric shrugged. "So sue me." He took a deep breath. "Barring unforeseen circumstances," he said slowly, "I cannot imagine ever running for any political office. That would be a twenty-four-hour-a-day job, and I already have a twenty-three-hour-a-day job that I find to be quite enough, thank you. Now is that better?"

The reporter shrugged, and Eric went on with the conference. When all the questions had been answered and Eric announced that the conference was over, Amanda positioned herself in front of WKM's cameras and closed her story: "At the close of today's conference Eric Harrison indicated that the focus of his investigation might go as high as the comptroller's office. Whether that will be the case remains to be seen. What is certain, however, is that the commission is looking into what may be one of the most scandalous developments in this city's history — a development that none of the networks is covering, perhaps an indication that faith in the integrity of government-appointed commissions is at such an all-time low that even the media have chosen to ignore conferences such as this one." Amanda sighed and called, "Cut." She shook her head and looked at the crew. "I'm sorry, Al, guys. We'll have to do that again."

"Looked good to me, Amanda," Al called from behind his camera.

Amanda shook her head. "Oh, thanks, Al, but it just wasn't right. The whole last part was just my opinion, an editorial." She laughed. "You're too used to the other stations, Al. I'm supposed to tell the truth. I'm sorry, but we'll have to do the whole thing over. Anyway, I think I stumbled over some of my words."

"I'd take a deep breath and count to ten before I did it again," drawled a smooth voice from the stage.

Amanda turned as Eric vaulted down from the platform.

He smiled and winked. "With those eyes you could speak gibberish and no one would really care, Miss WKM-TV. But if you really want to do it right, Amanda, relax, take a deep breath, and slow down. Speak as if you're talking with a friend, not as if you're racing a clock."

Amanda looked at him icily. "I *am* racing a clock, for your information," she flared. "I have only a forty-five-second sum-up thanks to the way the conference went. I'm including many more segments than I had planned."

Eric raised a dark brow. "But isn't that the point of the report? To show the conference, that is? Otherwise," he continued silkily, not quite suppressing a smile, "I'd have to as-

30

sume you were here to see me." His eyes grew serious, and when he spoke again, he spoke softly. "After seven years, Amanda. It's been a long time. It's good to see you."

"It's good to see you, too, Eric," she said quietly. Their eyes met, and suddenly Amanda felt as if she were being drawn toward those eyes, toward Eric, toward something she couldn't control. She stepped back and snapped out of the heated haze Eric's eyes had enveloped her in, and cleared her throat. "Okay," she said, turning to Al, "I know what I'm going to say in the sum-up now, so why don't we try it again, guys?"

"Do you want a dry run first, Amanda?" Al asked. "We've got time for it, you know."

"Uh-uh, it's okay," Amanda said, sounding much more confident than she really felt. With Eric's appreciative gaze taking her in from head to toe and back again, she could hardly concentrate on where she was, much less on what she was saying. As he stepped back and leaned against the stage, stretching his long legs out in front of him and crossing strong, solid arms with animal grace, he exuded an almost predatory masculinity, a challenge that reached her physically. It was as if, leaning back in relaxed confidence, he were saying, "Okay, you've

31

seen me handle an audience, now let's see just what you're made of."

Amanda swallowed and looked into the camera, which, mercifully, Al hadn't started rolling yet. "Uh, just a minute, Al. I think I need — I think I need a little more time."

"Sure thing," Al said comfortingly.

Amanda carried her notes to the far end of the stage, away from Eric. Damn him! One of her strongest talents was thinking and speaking on her feet, an essential skill for a reporter to have. And now she could hardly remember her own name! Well, she'd look at her notes, make a few new ones, and show Eric how good she was.

When she turned and walked back to her spot a few feet from Eric, he was standing in the same position, leaning rakishly against the stage, but he was now grinning broadly. "Don't worry," he drawled. "I'll catch you if your knees give way, and I won't tell Stan about any of this."

She shot him a look of disgust. "Go right ahead," she said coolly. "This isn't a bit unusual, at this sort of event." Her eyes fixed his. "What we call a 'low P.' "

He raised an eyebrow. "Low P?"

"Low priority," she answered. "Something we wouldn't cover if other, more important, stories came up." She turned to Al without waiting for a response from Eric. "Okay, Al, I'm ready now." And a minute later she had finished what she knew was an excellent sum-up: clear, to the point, and smoothly delivered. Although she hated to admit it, her success was in no small measure due to Eric. She had drawn upon all her mental and physical resources to face the challenging presence a few feet to her right: his flashing eyes, his lips curled in amusement, the mocking stance of his solid form had all dared her to be good.

She turned to Eric and he smiled broadly. "Well done, Amanda. Although you *did* blush every time you mentioned my name."

Her blue eyes flashed sparks of amused anger. "Eric Harrison," she said slowly, "if I thought that were true, I'd resign today. Forever," she cried.

He looked her up and down, slowly, assessingly, and then smiled. "To be with me, then? Abandon your career and all that?"

Amanda forced a laugh. He was joking about something that had been troubling her deeply lately — whether she would ever be able to have a strong and lasting relationship with a man now that her career was so all-consuming — and Eric was cutting close to the quick without realizing it. "Not quite," she said vaguely, turning to Al and the crew. She didn't want to think about the confusion and concern she read in Eric's deep brown eyes. "Well, guys. Al, do you think it went okay?"

"Great, Amanda." He grinned. "I may come around to your way of thinking yet. There wasn't a single joke in your segment, and it was pretty good, pretty good." He looked at his watch. "And now we're going to be pretty out of work if we don't get out of here."

"Oh, my God, you're right," Amanda cried, hoping no one had noticed the shrillness in her voice. Her time with Eric had been so short! "I'll be right out," she said to Al as the crew began rolling the equipment out.

When she turned to Eric, he was no longer smiling. A deep seriousness had darkened his brown eyes, and his lips were tight and thin. "I heard about your divorce, Amanda."

Amanda flushed; it had been a long, unpleasant process, and she knew the details had traveled far and wide. "Yes. Well, that was a long time ago," she said, trying to fathom Eric's expression. Why had he become so grim?

"Yes, I know," Eric said. "I, uh, spoke with

Greg the other day."

Amanda frowned. "Oh, really? Why?" she blurted out, realizing only after she had spoken that the answer wasn't necessarily any of her business.

"Ah, the reporter ever at work." He smiled. "Actually, it was — I asked him for some names — real-estate contacts." Eric frowned. "How is he, by the way, emotionally speaking? I couldn't really tell in the short time we spoke."

Amanda stared. "In — in what sense?" Eric's was an odd question, one that she neither knew how nor wanted to answer.

Eric shrugged. "I'm not quite sure. Greg always seemed a little — well, he's come a long way, Amanda, but somehow I can't help being surprised that he has."

Amanda's natural protectiveness for Greg was aroused. "You mean you're surprised that Greg has come a long way, although *your* success should come as no surprise to anyone?"

Eric cocked his head and knit his brows. "Now you know very well that's not what I meant. It's simply that Greg seems somehow . . . lost without you, and I'm surprised he's been able to handle himself as successfully as he evidently has in the years since the divorce. How many years has it been?"

"Five," Amanda said quickly, "and I'd really rather not discuss it right now, Eric."

"Of course," he said, looking into her eyes. "I'd forgotten how protective you always were of Greg. Old habits die hard, though, and you and I certainly did used to talk."

"Yes, well —"

"By the way," he said, narrowing his eyes, "the last I heard, you were doing lost-dog stories up in Albany."

Amanda laughed. "Where did you hear that?"

"I have my spies," he said smoothly. "But seriously, Amanda, you're not taking over the political scene for WKM, are you?"

"City politics, yes," she said, uneasy over a certain quality in his voice. Was it doubt? "Why?" she prodded.

He sighed and shifted position. "Is that what you really want?"

Amanda rolled her eyes. "I've been asked that question about a hundred times in the past week, Eric, and I doubt if anyone would even think of asking it if I were a man."

His eyes sparkled. "Well, most clearly and spectacularly you're not. But I *would* like to know what your intentions are, and why."

Amanda sighed. "It's simply a question of significance, I guess. It's not that I think human-interest stories are less important or less interesting, Eric. But for now what's significant to *me*, what I can do best, is politics. And I think I have an unjaundiced eye that'll be good for the station." She smiled. "You know as well as I do that most of the political reporters in this town are hard-bitten, hard-drinking guys who know what they're talking about, but who've been taking the same approach for years. Maybe too many years."

Eric frowned. "Then you intend to continue WKM's coverage of the commission."

"Yes," Amanda exclaimed. "And it'll be great, with my knowing you." She smiled. "I'll have the best inside source there is. All my news straight from the horse's mouth."

Eric didn't return the smile. In fact, he looked almost pained. "Amanda, I — I don't think politics is your area." He cleared his throat. "Your sum-up was excellent, there's no doubt about that. But I know you, Amanda, and your talents — *I* feel, at least — would show up more clearly in another area."

"Just what area did you have in mind?" she snapped. "Cooking lessons, perhaps? Maybe reading off the weather? Something more 'feminine'?"

He smiled sadly. "I'm sorry, Amanda. I

meant no such thing. I'm obviously not making myself clear."

"You always did do better with a large audience," she parried.

"Oh, you're all the audience I need, Amanda. It's simply that —" He paused. "It's simply that I wish you would give this story to someone else. That's all I can say. It would be so much easier." He sighed and shook his head. "Well, I can see I'm not getting through to you. And who knows? I might be wrong about something anyway," he said mysteriously, and then brightened. "Let's just forget I said anything at all about your career, Amanda. Now, would you like to —"

"Amanda!" boomed Al's voice from the doorway.

"I have to go," Amanda said. "I'll see you at your next press conference, Eric. I intend to be there, even if you think I belong somewhere else."

Eric put strong hands on her shoulders and looked into her eyes. "Don't misunderstand me, Amanda."

She tried to ignore the heat of Eric's hands, the weakness of her knees, the warmth coursing through her as he held her so firmly. Taking a deep breath, she coldly and carefully removed his hands from her shoulders. "And don't patronize *me,* Eric. If you don't think I'm the right person to cover this story, well, that's your opinion. But I don't share it, and neither does my boss." She shook her head. "I'm only sorry I didn't know how you felt about me professionally when we — when we knew each other seven years ago. Good-bye."

She turned and walked quickly to the door, ignoring him as he called her name.

Chapter Two

Later that afternoon, as Amanda sat in the editing room running through the footage of the press conference, she watched with a sinking heart as the events of the afternoon were repeated before her eyes moment by moment. Al had had the cameras rolling for virtually every minute of the conference, and now Amanda had no choice but to sit and watch Eric for frame after agonizing frame.

He was extremely photogenic, as it turned out; his dark good looks were accentuated by the lights Amanda's crew had set up.

"Amanda," said Vivian, the film editor, sitting next to her in the darkness, "you really lucked out on your first assignment. That guy is gorgeous! Carlotta usually sticks the new reporters — if they're young and female, that is — with stories no one else would want to touch in a million years. But wow, he's really something!"

Amanda smiled ruefully. "Yes, he is. On the outside, at least."

Vivian looked up sharply. "You know him?"

"I used to," Amanda said glumly.

"Looks as if you knew him well, Amanda, from the way he — hey, what's the matter? Did I say something wrong?"

Amanda shook her head. "No, that's okay. I'm just a little preoccupied. I guess I did know Eric well, Vivian, but not in the sense you might expect. I was a paralegal at his law firm years ago" — she smiled — "my first job out of college. And we got to know each other pretty well. Something just clicked between us. It seemed as if every Monday morning when we came in to work, we'd discover either that we had done and liked the same things — like movies and plays — or that we had had the same kind of problems at home. And it was funny, because now that I think back, it wasn't that we actually discussed our problems very much — we were both very private people — but there was always an undercurrent, an 'I understand,' going back and forth between us."

"Did you — well, kick me if you don't think I should ask, but did you have an affair?"

Amanda shook her head. "No. We were both married then. He still is, as far as I know."

Vivian rolled her eyes. "He sure doesn't act married on this tape, Amanda. Look at the way he's looking at you."

Amanda turned and watched, hypnotized, as Eric appeared in a new clip on the monitor. She hadn't known Al had been running the camera when she had first come face to face with Eric, but there it was on the screen: Amanda telling Al she'd have to do her sum-up, and then Eric vaulting down from the stage, smiling and saying, "With those eyes you could speak gibberish and no one would really care . . ." and, to Amanda's horror as clear as day, a deepening blush rising on her cheeks as Eric looked at her.

"Will you look at that guy move?" Vivian said. "He moves just like a tiger." Suddenly she leaned forward and flipped a switch, and Eric was moving in slow motion, fluidly stepping back against the stage, looking Amanda over assessingly — inch by inch — from head to toe, taking in her eyes, her breasts, her legs, her eyes again, his own eyes gleaming with desire and obvious approval. As he stretched out his legs and shifted position, Amanda was mesmerized by the powerful muscles in his arms, the obvious muscularity of his legs, the tensile strength of his entire body. He was as relaxed as only an athlete can be, in total control of every fiber of muscle in his lean body.

Vivian flipped the switch back as the

camera shifted out of Eric's field. "Well," she laughed, "that was certainly more interesting than what comes next."

"Thanks a lot. I hope Stan likes my script better than you do."

"Oh, it's fine, Amanda, it just can't compare to a gorgeous guy with a perfect body doing slow-motion acrobatics, that's all."

Amanda laughed. "Well, seriously, though, let's cut it so it's as good as it can possibly be. I want to stay on this story more than you can imagine."

"Oh, I can imagine, Amanda. I'd want to stay on it, too."

Amanda smiled and shook her head. "No, Vivian. For a *different* reason. And this is why I'm so — I don't know if I'm hurt or angry or both. But Eric doesn't think the story is 'right' for me. I don't know why not, but he — it was practically like saying he thought I was an okay reporter, but not very good. And not good enough for *his* story, in any event."

Vivian frowned. "I don't know, Amanda. He certainly isn't looking at you as if he thinks you're any kind of inferior." She shook her head. "You must have misunderstood him." She shrugged. "But don't worry. We'll make this so great Stan *and* Eric Harrison will flip. I guarantee it."

"Great," Amanda said. "I really appreciate your help, Vivian." She glanced at the monitor and looked away quickly. "I don't know why I'm still feeling edgy, but I am." The more she looked at Eric — at his easy camaraderie with the reporters, his fluid grace, the masculinity he simply possessed rather than flaunted or exaggerated — the more unhappy she felt. She couldn't deny the impact he had on her physically. Almost every time she looked at him, her body warmed and weakened as she thought of the hungry kiss they had shared, of the heated but restrained dozens and dozens of touches they had shared years earlier: hands brushing, hips grazing, eyes locking in gazes that seemed as if they could never end. She hadn't planned on being able to ignore her physical reactions to Eric, as the connection was simply too powerful, too deep. But she had hoped — indeed, assumed — that she could set her feelings aside and have a friendly relationship that would be good for them both professionally, as well as satisfying in its own right.

But Eric had turned everything upside down, in a totally unexpected way, by showing an aspect of his personality she had never before known and he had shocked her and hurt her by so doing. She *knew* she was a good reporter — a damn good one. And even if WKM was the lowest-rated of all the news shows in New York City, it was still New York, after all, and hers was one of the most sought-after jobs in the country. She knew she had worked for and deserved it, and she didn't doubt her own ability. Why, then, did he?

Later in the afternoon, as Amanda and Vivian and Stan Daniels watched the edited clip come to an end, Amanda silently dared Eric to watch her report tonight without changing his mind about her. Through careful cutting and splicing, editing and re-editing, Vivian had created a fast-paced clip that made Amanda look as cool as a cucumber and made Eric look like a political genius.

When the clip was over, Vivian switched off the monitor and turned on the lights. Stan looked at Amanda and shook his head. "I've gotta hand it to you, Amanda. That was one fine report. Really fine. And knowing Eric, you can be sure there'll be lots of follow-up work. You'll be going to a lot more press conferences on the Harrison Commission without a doubt."

"Yes," Amanda said vaguely, wondering whether she should tell Stan about Eric's not wanting her to cover the story anymore.

But she decided — for then, at least — to say nothing; whatever the source of Eric's feelings, it was a personal matter, and one that could stay personal as long as it didn't interfere with her impartial coverage of the story.

Stan studied Amanda, then leaned back and folded his hands across his rather large stomach. "You know, Amanda, Al told me that you and Eric know each other." He shifted his bulky frame into a more comfortable position. "Now, Eric and I go back a long way. I haven't spoken to him in years, but we're good, solid old friends." He smiled. "Poker buddies from way back, as a matter of fact."

Amanda nodded absently, dreading and wondering what Stan was leading up to.

"Anyway," Stan continued, looking from Vivian to Amanda, "what do you think of our doing a close-up on Eric? You know, in our Friday night slot."

"Oh, no," Amanda blurted, instantly wishing she hadn't spoken so quickly.

Stan was studying her as if trying to figure out if she were ill or not, and Vivian was trying to suppress a laugh.

"I don't understand," Stan said. "Obviously the commission is up to something. Eric has never spent a day in his life without being 'up to something.' And you know the man, Amanda. Why —"

"I think it's a super idea," Vivian interrupted. "As an impartial observer and a very partial editor, Amanda, I can tell you I'd love to see you do it."

Amanda glared warningly at Vivian and then turned to Stan. What could she say? Professionally, she'd be a fool to turn down an offer like this one — and she wouldn't dream of turning it down only because Eric didn't want her to pursue the story. But she had to consider the station's needs, and she simply didn't think that she'd be able to get as much information out of Eric as any of the other reporters. "I'm sorry, Stan, I —"

"I won't take no for an answer," Stan interrupted. "And anyway, Amanda, you and Eric are perfect for each other. You could get a story that —" He suddenly paled. "Oh, no," he said, shaking his head. "I've done it again." He looked at Amanda and smiled sheepishly. "My wife has told me a thousand times — in situations just like this — to keep my big fat mouth shut, and I've done it again."

Amanda and Vivian looked at each other, mystified, and turned back to Stan. "What do you mean?" Amanda asked.

"It's obvious," Stan said, "and I'm sorry. When Al said you and Eric knew each other,

I hadn't realized that — well, you know, that — you might have man-woman problems. You know."

Amanda held herself back from smiling; for a hard-drinking, two-fisted news director, Stan was certainly acting coy. And how wrong he was! "And that's what you — ?" She widened her eyes. "If *that's* why you think I don't want to do the story — and you couldn't be farther from the truth — well, you've just signed me up, Stan." She teasingly shook a finger at him. "I'm surprised that by now you don't know you shouldn't say something like that to a woman and not expect her to do something about it." She narrowed her eyes, but with a smile. "Would you assume a man couldn't handle a situation like this?"

Stan shrugged. "Well, I —"

Amanda laughed. "Never mind. But I'll do the story, Stan," she said, trying to block the image of Eric out of her mind. "I promise you that."

"Great," Stan said. "I may even give Eric a call myself." He winked. "Just to help things along a bit. I understand he's pretty close-mouthed about the investigation at this point."

Amanda nodded. "Very."

Stan shifted in his chair. "Well," he

smiled, "maybe it's about time I rustled up our old poker game again. I imagine he's got some more time on his hands now that Jillian's gone. 'Don't speak ill of the dead' and all that, but hell, she dragged him to more society events in one month than Prince Charles goes to in a year."

Amanda paled. "Did you say 'dead'?"

Stan knit his brows and took a deep breath. "I thought you knew." He sighed and looked away. "I'm sorry," he said. "I thought —"

"Never mind," Amanda interrupted. "But how did she die?"

"In a plane crash. A private plane. With Tom Sievert, from —"

"My God, I *know* Tom Sievert. From Eric's office! What — how did it happen?"

Stan shook his head. "I don't know the details. Except that the plane crashed into the side of a mountain. In Vermont."

"When did this happen?"

"Six, seven months ago."

Amanda simply stared. Jillian was dead. With Tom Sievert, whom Amanda had hardly known, but still, how awful!

"Well." Stan's voice broke through Amanda's thoughts. He slapped his thighs and stood up. "It's all food for thought, but we do have a news show to produce, so let's break it up." He pointed at Amanda. "And I expect you to start laying the groundwork for the close-up on Eric, Amanda. We'll set Friday after next as air date."

"Got it," she said gamely, trying to feel half as confident as she sounded. She gave Stan a mock salute and went back through the newsroom to her office, a tiny glassed-in cubicle at the edge of a room that was in total chaos as usual.

When she sat down at her desk, she took out her folder of notes on Eric and began reading through them. But it was impossible for her to concentrate, and she read the words without understanding.

Eric was alone now — though not literally, Amanda was certain; he probably had several girl friends.

She remembered, with guilt, how Jillian and Greg were all that had prevented her and Eric from having an affair those seven years ago. The looks of longing, the stolen moments of touching, the conversations that were more undercurrent than words — heated minutes, hours, and days of fantasies they each knew the other shared. Now Jillian was dead, and Greg was . . . well, Greg: dependent, immature, perpetually unhappy. Amanda felt she had changed in many ways. She had carved out a career for

50

herself, grown up enough to be able to say "No, enough" loudly and clearly to Greg, matured enough to know that what she wanted from a relationship was more than friendship, more than physical love, more even than the sum of the two parts; and she also suspected — deeply, in the parts of her heart and mind she tried to ignore — that what she wanted would never be possible.

And it was disturbing to see that now that Eric was no longer married, now that she was free to do anything and everything she wanted, now that all of the "obstacles" had been removed, what was she left with? Here was a situation she had dreamed of seven years ago (although she hadn't wanted Jillian to die) — and the reality was almost as empty as the fantasy had been promising. Eric was more attractive than ever — infuriatingly so. Yet he was distant, acting in a way he never would have seven years ago.

One of the many things that had drawn Amanda and Eric together so closely was a mutual faith in each other, an unconditional support that had buoyed each of them up on the most discouraging of days. Amanda could remember how an attorney at the firm had falsely accused her of losing a document she had never even seen, and although she defended herself as well as she could, it was Eric — office politics being what they were — who had straightened the situation out. And when Eric lost a case he had cared about deeply, Amanda sat and talked with him for hours about anything and everything. And when he had finally looked at her, taking her hands in his, and said, "I think you know why we can't go on like this," they each looked into the other's eyes and knew they were not alone in the way they felt.

At least, that was what Amanda had *thought.* Yet perhaps it had all been a fantasy, an elaborate product of an overactive imagination. Amanda now felt a deep sense of loss, but somehow it was more than loss; she had just lost something she had never even had. Her life was even emptier now than she had ever imagined; something she had cherished and comforted herself with — the memory of a relationship — had never existed at all.

The ringing of the phone on her desk cut through Amanda's thoughts and brought her back to the tumult of the newsroom. She answered on the second ring. "Newsroom, Amanda Ellis speaking."

There was a silence, then a sigh. "I never will get used to that name, Amanda."

"Hello, Greg," she said. "How are you?"

She closed her eyes and waited for the usual onslaught, a river of sad complaints and subtle and not-so-subtle accusations, a note of blame present in each syllable and pause.

"I'm okay," Greg said noncommittally, and surprisingly. "Business is great." His tone sounded as if he had just told her he was going bankrupt.

"Well, you don't sound okay," she heard herself say, and then wished she hadn't. After all, this conversational pattern was exactly what had doomed their marriage almost from the start, making Amanda feel as if she were being pulled under again and again by Greg's needs.

"Oh, you know," he said vaguely. "Life could be better. But I really just called to congratulate you, Amanda."

She smiled. "Well, thanks. I'd been meaning to tell you about the job, but I've been really busy what with the new job and settling in to the new apartment and all —"

"Where is it?" he cut in.

"Uh, Eighty-eighth and Riverside," she said slowly, wishing she didn't feel strangely uneasy telling this to Greg. "It's really nice."

"Why didn't you let me help, Amanda? You know I could have gotten you something better."

Amanda sighed. "I know, Greg, and

thanks. But I didn't want something 'better.' I like where I am. And I wanted to keep it all simple. You know."

"Yeah, I know," he said in a changed, rough voice. "Just like you always kept things simple. Like with that Eric Harrison and Jeff Parks and —"

"Stop it, Greg," she cut in.

She could hear the sound of ice clinking in a glass. "Sorry," he said gruffly, and paused. "I saw Harrison, by the way. Today."

"Oh, really?" she said, mentally patting herself on the back for not having told Greg that she already knew. That little piece of information would undoubtedly create a string of totally inaccurate scenarios in Greg's mind that could make things difficult for everyone concerned.

"Yeah, he needed some names for this inquiry he's making, some commission. I gave him some help," he said, and waited as if expecting Amanda to thank him or tell him he had done well. She said nothing.

"Just tell me one thing," he said aggressively.

"What's that?" she asked, dreading his next words.

"Just tell me I didn't give any help today

to someone my wife cheated on me with seven years ago."

Amanda closed her eyes. Why was this happening to her? She felt as if she were married to Greg again, back in the same conflicts, the same circular arguments, the same endless battles that went nowhere. "Greg, I have a job to do, a life to live, and I simply won't have you dragging me back into something that's over. No, I never had an affair with Eric, but for you to ask now is" — she shook her head — "if you don't understand, you never will."

"I'm sorry, Amanda, I —"

"I'm sorry, too, Greg. I do want to keep in touch, and you know that. But not if . . . not if it doesn't work out."

He sighed, and she could hear him take another sip of whatever he was drinking. "Listen, Amanda, I *am* sorry. I didn't want — all I wanted to do was congratulate you."

She nodded. "And the congratulations are accepted, Greg. Thanks."

"But listen, Amanda, the office is pretty hectic so I'll have to sign off now."

"Okay, Greg," she said placatingly, allowing him to pretend — probably to himself most of all — that he wanted or needed to end the conversation.

"I'll watch you on the tube tonight. WKM, right?"

"Right. Bye."

After she hung up, she closed her eyes and leaned back in her chair. She felt as angry as she always did after her conversations with Greg — angry at herself for being unable to cut the tie, and at Greg for going through the same motions he had been going through for years. But she couldn't totally abandon him. He needed her, and while she simply cared for him now, she had once loved him.

And that fact was the most difficult to believe, to understand, to face. Because if she had once been sure Greg was the one — and she had been certain then — how could she ever be sure again? And would she ever meet anyone whom she would even have cause to wonder about?

Amanda's speculations were cut short by the shift in activity in the newsroom outside her office. Except for the young woman handling the wire services, and the night-shift employees who had just arrived, everyone was gathered around the monitors set into the wall outside Stan's office. It was almost six o'clock, and the news was about to begin.

Amanda took a deep breath and walked

out into the newsroom to join her colleagues. All fifteen or so people were gathered on and around the desks outside Stan's office, with Stan in the middle of the group. Amanda sat down at the edge of the group as the theme music came on, and then Jeremy Sanford, the anchorman, appeared on screen. Amanda listened vaguely to his announcements of the broadcasts to come, and suddenly he was saying, "And our new correspondent, Amanda Ellis, will have a report on the newly formed Harrison Commission, investigating corruption in city-licensing practices."

"Right on!" Vivian called out, and Stan winked at Amanda.

Amanda half listened and half watched the rest of the broadcast, and then suddenly Eric appeared on screen, with Amanda superimposed with a microphone in front of him. Her heart skipped a beat and then pounded wildly as she watched the report, aware that everyone around her had stopped joking and talking; they were ready to see and hear the new correspondent. And to judge her as well, she realized.

But the report was over only seconds later, and people were saying, "Congratulations, Amanda," and "That was really great," all around her. Stan shushed everybody, and a moment later the group returned to its former half quiet.

Amanda was immensely relieved that everyone had liked the report, and that it had stood up to Stan's tough scrutiny a second time. Yet her triumph felt strangely lonely. She had no one to share it with, just as she had had no one truly close with whom to share her news of the job at WKM. Her parents had died in a boating accident a year ago, and since then Amanda hadn't had anyone cheering her on. It was strange, really, that after having decided to devote herself almost entirely to her career, she had ironically and unhappily discovered that without someone to share one's triumphs, almost all successes have an empty ring to them.

A young woman tapped on Amanda's arm and nodded in the direction of the switchboard operator. Amanda stood up as the woman signaled for her to take a call in her office.

Amanda knew it had to be Greg, upset over the way their phone call had gone; he often called two and three times in a row.

Amanda answered with resignation and cynicism in her voice. "Newsroom. Amanda Ellis speaking."

But it was an altogether different voice

that answered. "Yes," Eric said smoothly. "I'm looking for a rather stubborn, very attractive reporter from your station. A very fast runner, too, I might add. She ran out on my press conference before I could ask her out to dinner."

Amanda smiled. "As I recall, the press conference was over, Mr. Harrison."

"But I was far from finished with you, Amanda," he said softly, and then laughed. "And I can *hear* you blushing."

"Oh, I am *not.*" Amanda insisted, trying to stop herself from laughing.

"Well, you would be blushing if you knew what I was thinking, Amanda." He paused. "You looked beautiful today. You've changed more than I had ever imagined."

"Oh, well, thank you so much," she said drily. "That doesn't speak very well of my earlier years, Eric."

He laughed softly. "Oh, no, Amanda. You can't play that game with me, and you know what I meant: You used to be shaped rather . . . differently, shall we say. But either way is fine with me." He paused. "You can't have forgotten how I used to feel about you, Amanda. We could hardly keep our hands off each other."

Amanda tried to ignore the feeling of warmth that was flowing through her. She had to bring the conversation back to safer ground. She cleared her throat. "Um, I spoke to Greg this afternoon, by the way."

"And — ?" His tone was sharp.

Amanda was mystified by Eric's strong reaction. "What do you mean, 'and'? I spoke to Greg, that's all. You *did* ask how he was, and . . . never mind," she said, exasperated. What was Eric being so touchy about?

"Did he mention his having spoken with me?" Eric demanded roughly.

"Well, yes, as a matter of fact, he did."

There was a silence. Then Eric muttered something Amanda couldn't quite hear, and cleared his throat. "Goddamn it, Amanda, that is precisely the type of situation I wanted to avoid, and precisely why I asked you not to work on the story. That we used to know each other, and . . . well, that we used to know each other simply puts too many complications into an already complicated situation. It just won't work."

"I don't understand," Amanda said slowly. "I'm certainly not taking advantage of the situation, and why are you so upset that Greg and I have spoken? He —"

"Amanda," Eric interrupted, "you're not listening to me. My investigation is confidential, and any leak — any leak from any source — could be critical. I didn't mind your knowing I had consulted with Greg, but he certainly didn't have the go-ahead to reveal that fact — even to you. You're a reporter, for one thing — not just his ex-wife." He paused. "I'm sorry, Amanda," he said softly, "but I think it would be better from now on if we stayed out of touch until the investigation is over. I'm more sorry than you can imagine." He sighed. "I can't say good-bye without telling you, though — you looked beautiful in your report tonight. Good-bye, Amanda."

And he hung up before she could say a word.

Chapter Three

The next morning, when Amanda arrived at work, Stan waved her in as she passed by his office.

Amanda stepped in with some trepidation. She had hardly slept the night before, tossing and turning as she wondered how she was ever going to get a decent story on Eric now that he didn't even want to speak with her until the commission was finished. And she wondered whether she was professionally obligated to let Stan know of her doubts and difficulties at this point. Of course, perhaps he would be able to help, but more likely still he would feel that she had gotten herself embroiled in a sticky problem she had no business being involved in — perhaps an indication of an unexpected lack of professionalism.

Now, as she pulled up a chair in front of Stan's desk, she was glad she had decided to keep her problems to herself, at least for now. Stan was impatiently tapping a pencil on his desk, looking steadily at Amanda with an expression she couldn't read.

When she sat down, he leaned forward. "I thought of another angle." He pursed his lips. "You know, at this point, WKM has scooped all the other stations on the Harrison Commission." He smiled. "NBC had a segment this morning. But we can't be satisfied with that one scoop on this story. So" — he steepled his fingers — "what I want from you, Amanda, is a really in-depth look at Eric, and I want you to concentrate on his political aspirations. I think he's a shoo-in for the Democratic nomination for the Senate, and it'd sure be nice if we were first on record with that as well."

Amanda swallowed. "Yes. Well. It certainly would be nice." She flashed a smile she hoped looked more sincere than it felt. "If that's all, Stan, I'll be on my way."

He shrugged and gave her a mock salute. "That's all for now. Except that I'm glad you're the one on the story, Amanda. I know you'll do a superb job."

Back in her office, Amanda dialed Eric's office without letting her skepticism get the better of her. She had no idea what sort of reception she would be greeted with at the other end of the line by his staff, but there was only one way to find out. To her surprise, Amanda's mention of the profile on Eric was greeted with wild enthusiasm by a young-sounding voice who introduced herself as Sheila Farnham, Eric's press aide and assistant. Sheila invited Amanda to come by that morning, and Amanda was beginning to feel that perhaps Eric had spoken yesterday in the heat of the moment and had since reconsidered.

When she arrived at Eric's commission office down near City Hall, Amanda was immediately struck by the seriousness of the operation. A far cry from Eric's usual plush office in Rockefeller Center, the room — a large office at the end of a run-down hall in an equally run-down building — was bustling with activity. Young men and women were busily typing and talking on the phone, and charts and pieces of paper tacked onto virtually every inch of wall space bespoke the high level of activity that had apparently been going on since well before the press conference.

A young woman who was on the phone at an overflowing desk in the corner of the room waved Amanda over, and signaled she'd be off the phone in a moment.

Amanda went over and sat across from the young woman, assuming she was a young volunteer or a college intern. She looked about twenty or twenty-one, with curly blond hair, pretty brown eyes, and a liveliness Amanda hadn't seen in a long time. Everyone at the newsrooms she had been working in for the past years had been infused with a different kind of energy, one that was somehow cynical and less cheerful.

The young woman finally hung up. She smiled and rolled her eyes. "Well, sorry to keep you waiting," she apologized, standing up and extending her hand. "I'm Sheila Farnham, Miss Ellis, Eric's press aide and assistant."

"Oh," Amanda said, startled. "Nice to meet you." Lord, she was so young! They shook hands and sat down.

Sheila smiled. "You did a beautiful job on that report the other day, Miss Ellis. We loved it. Everyone in the office was ecstatic afterward."

Amanda looked at her steadily. "Well, thank you, Sheila —"

"I mean," Sheila interrupted, "I know that Eric is the one who really makes it special — no offense or anything. Everything he's in just looks so wonderful. But it's nice to have someone on our side, so to speak."

Amanda frowned. "On your side?"

Sheila shrugged. "Well, we both know that's not supposed to be true, but Eric told me you two knew each other pretty well a few years ago, so —"

"Miss Farnham," Amanda began gently, "I realize that enthusiasm for one's job can sometimes cloud one's vision, and you're obviously as enthusiastic about your job as anyone can get. But please don't misunderstand the situation, especially at this crucial time. Eric and I may have once been friends, but that fact will never color my coverage of him." She wondered whether this was in fact true, but went on nevertheless: "It's important that you understand that."

Sheila looked crestfallen. "I see," she said slowly. "I'm sorry for what I said. Please forgive me." She looked at Amanda with imploring brown eyes. "And please don't tell Eric what I said. He'll kill me if he finds out."

Amanda looked at her with surprise. "You're his press aide, Sheila. He's obviously put a lot of trust in you — for a reason."

Sheila shrugged. "Well, I have to be extra careful now what with all the political talk. The whole job has become a lot more complicated now that Eric has pretty much thrown his glove into the political ring."

Amanda frowned. "That wasn't my understanding," she said. "About the political question, that is. Sheila, you saw and heard that section of my report. Eric very clearly stated that he was not going to seek nomination for any political office.'"

Sheila smiled and shook her head. "Uh-uh, not if you listened very carefully, Miss Ellis." She suddenly looked quite pleased with herself. "What Eric said — twice — at the conference was that he had no 'plans' to seek political office. But he didn't say it wouldn't happen."

"I take it that those are *your* plans for him in any case, Miss Farnham."

Sheila shrugged. "I guess it's impossible for me to say no at this point. Yes, I have big plans for Eric." She gestured at the rest of the office. "You'll find that we all do here at the commission because we all know what he can do."

Amanda looked past Sheila to the wall behind her desk, where a series of eight-by-ten glossy photos of Eric were tacked up. They were undeniably well-done, varied head and upper-body shots of Eric in some outdoor setting. He was smiling in some, thoughtful and serious in others, and unsettlingly seductive in the photo at the center of the group. Amanda wouldn't have believed it possible to capture that look to such an extent in a photograph, but Eric seemed actually to be staring at her from the photo, his deep dark eyes penetrating hers with a

67

heated look that was frankly sexual. The corners of his mouth were curved in a look that seemed to say, "I know what you're thinking . . . and I'm thinking the same thing," but that also mocked at the same time. His collar was open with the shirt unbuttoned just enough to expose a few curls of dark hair and the strength of his neck, and Amanda was suddenly swept up in a flood of memories of that one kiss she and Eric had shared.

"Oh," Sheila's voice interrupted her thoughts. "Those pictures." She smiled. "I took those when Eric and I were upstate this summer. At the state capital."

"Oh, really," Amanda observed, keeping the surprise out of her voice as well as she could. "Well, they're certainly nice."

"Nice enough to be campaign posters, don't you think?"

Amanda shrugged. "I suppose, if that's what Eric wants."

"*I* certainly think they're good enough, if I do say so myself. All except for the one in the center. I don't think the voters would go for anyone that overtly seductive." Sheila looked past Amanda, and her face lit up. "Well, home comes the hunter!" she cried out merrily, and Amanda turned to follow Sheila's gaze.

As if the center photograph had come alive, Eric strode across the room, wearing the same open-necked white shirt that hugged his shoulders and upper chest and tapered down to his narrow hips. His hair was disheveled, a thick dark lock defiantly hanging down over stormy eyes, and his purposeful stride made him look angrier still. His dark eyes flashed at Amanda and locked her in a gaze that took her breath away.

Suddenly he was standing over her, his massive arms folded and lean legs planted squarely apart, raw anger emanating from every inch of his tall frame. "Is this your idea of dropping a story?" he demanded, his voice hoarse with fury.

"For your information," Amanda flared, "my presence here has little if anything to do with your commission, Mr. Harrison," she snapped. "I've been assigned to do an in-depth close-up on you." She took in a deep breath of air. "For airing the Friday after next."

The corners of his hard mouth curved upward into a smile and then broadened into a grin. He threw back his dark head and laughed.

Amanda stood up, her cheeks flaming. Taking a deep breath, she put her hands firmly on Eric's upper arms and said, "Maybe I'll skip the profile, Eric. It was Stan's idea — not mine."

Suddenly there wasn't even a glimmer of a smile on Eric's face, as deep brown met pale blue in a searching gaze that made Amanda's heart race. She took her hands away from his shoulders; the gesture had had the desired effect — to stop him from laughing and embarrassing her in front of his whole staff — and there was no reason to keep touching him, was there? But Eric looked down at her hands as she removed them from his shoulders, and when he looked into her eyes again, his eyes were asking her a question she was glad would remain unspoken. He had noticed her touch — a movement inappropriate coming from a newswoman he barely knew, but all too appropriate coming from a woman with whom he had shared fantasies and deep desires years earlier. Was it an intimacy, he wondered, that would lead to more? A first step on a long sensual path toward the fulfillment of years of yearning?

Amanda broke the hold of Eric's gaze by looking past him. "So, Mr. Harrison," she said crisply, "the choice is yours to make." Then she met his eyes with challenge. "I recommend that you set aside whatever no-tions you have that have led you to balk at this . . . opportunity. But if, for whatever reason, you choose not to take up WKM on this project" — she shrugged — "I can't promise future coverage at any level."

He looked at her with cool menace. "Is that a threat?" he hazarded silkily.

She frowned. "I wouldn't say so, no. Although it could certainly be interpreted that way. It's simply a question of loyalties, I suppose."

He raised a dark brow. "Meaning — ?"

"Meaning that if you cut WKM out at this point in what may or may not be an illustrious career, I can't answer for what WKM's position will be toward you in the future. News is news, of course, but politics is something else. If you *are* embarking on a political career," she said drily, glancing at an open-mouthed Sheila Farnham, "I suggest you give our proposition some thought."

He barely suppressed a smile. "I see," he stated. "An interesting dilemma." He gestured toward a door to his left. "And interesting dilemmas, my dear Brenda Starr, always require long, slow, careful thought." His eyes gleamed. "And sometimes discussion with a friend doesn't hurt, either. Follow me?" And he turned and led her into his small, cluttered office, as different from the office she had shared with Eric those seven years ago as could be.

Fifteen minutes later Amanda was sitting with Eric in the back seat of a cab heading up Central Park West, having acceded to his demand for "more pleasant surroundings."

"Have you ever been to Tavern on the Green?" Eric asked.

Amanda smiled and shook her head. "No. I've wanted to go for years, but somehow the occasion has never been right." She looked at Eric. "It's a long way from your office, though, at least for lunch."

"Ah, well . . ." He looked at her steadily. "I believe in doing things right, Amanda. And that means going all the way every time." He smiled. "Figuratively, of course. Which means that if I decide to take an attractive reporter out to lunch, I'll take her only to what I think is the perfect place for a lunch of this sort." He reached out and ran a forefinger from her temple along the edge of her cheek down to her chin. Her lips parted as she looked into his eyes. "And I believe in finishing what I start, Amanda. Which means that now that I've agreed to speak with you" — he grinned — "to bare my deepest, darkest secrets, you'll have to be there to listen. If it's going to be 'in-depth,' as you said." He gently brushed her bangs aside. "Now that I'm free to talk . . . and you're free to listen."

Amanda tried to smile in an attempt to lighten the mood. The atmosphere had suddenly become charged with unspoken questions she wasn't ready to answer, and Eric's gestures — grazing her cheek, brushing back her hair — were raising more questions still. "Eric," Amanda began, edging slightly away from him on the seat, "it's . . . well, this *is* an interview, you know." She smiled. "I don't think WKM's viewers will be particularly interested in our . . . how can I say it? In the details of our new relationship."

Eric shifted position on the seat so that his knee touched hers; its heat was all she could think about. "And we don't even know what the relationship is yet, do we?" he murmured, looking into her eyes with a look that sent a warm rush of desire through her. "Or do we?" he added softly.

"I —"

Eric reached over and took her hand in his, never taking his eyes from hers. He laced his strong fingers through hers, and then gently let go as he lightly brushed the palm of her hand with his fingertips, in slow circles that gradually shifted upward until he was running his hand along her arm in a heated path that seemed to awaken parts of her body he hadn't even touched. "I haven't forgotten," he said huskily, as his hand traveled up to the smooth hollow of her neck and down along her collar, two fingers searing cool flesh and setting it afire. "I haven't forgotten what we wanted so much, Amanda, and neither have you," he continued quietly. "No one could forget something they wanted that much."

Amanda couldn't say anything. She was caught in the slow rhythm of Eric's caress, the deliberate leisurely circles his fingers traced along the curve of her neck, the rise of her breasts, caught, too, by the strong pressure of his leg that she so wanted to touch, to caress and press to her aching body as she had fantasized so many times. . . . And here he was, the man she had dreamed of so many times — his muscular thighs outlined in obvious detail through his tightly fitting pants — whose hair her cheeks had caressed in fantasy, whose chest she had kissed in dreams.

Amanda took a deep breath, grasped Eric's hand, and put it firmly down on his leg. "Eric," she said, surprised she had found her voice after forcing herself to return to reality, "I really don't think that this is . . . exactly what we should be doing. Or talking about. WKM doesn't pay me to —"

"To make love in the back seat of taxis going through Central Park?"

She laughed. "Well, we weren't quite doing that."

He sighed and shook his head. "Much to my regret. I should have taken you to lunch in Vermont." He fixed her with his eyes. "That takes four hours — which is about how long —"

"Eric, " Amanda cut in, laughing despite her attempt to bring the conversation back to its proper level. "I'm serious."

"So am I," he said quietly. "More than you can imagine." His eyes held hers with the promise that he was speaking the truth.

She sighed and looked away. When she looked back at Eric, his eyes met hers immediately. "Eric, you're not making this situation any easier."

"I'm not trying to, particularly." He looked from her eyes to her hair to her mouth, and back to her eyes again. "I'm feeling my way as much as you are. We had something very special seven years ago, something you can't pretend didn't happen. And I'm not going to let our meeting together just slip past without . . . without testing it, seeing what's there."

"It's chance that we met again, Eric," Amanda said firmly. "Look at the facts. You didn't call me. I didn't call you. It's been seven years."

"You thought I was married," he stated. "And I was . . . until recently. Amanda, we're not kids. We're two adults who had a spectacularly suppressed relationship seven years ago. My God, the number of times I sent you out of the office just because I knew I'd have to touch you if you stayed one more second." He laughed and shook his head. "Don't pretend it didn't happen then, Amanda, and don't ignore it now." He shrugged. "I won't let you even if you try."

Amanda shifted so that she was directly facing Eric; somehow she could never say what she meant — and had never been able to — if she was touching him in any way. "Now listen to me, Eric," she said firmly, shaking a finger at him. "I'm not playing around. It's all well and good for you to talk about our 'spectacularly suppressed relationship' and make intimations about what may or may not come to pass in the future. But let me explain something to you clearly, once and for all. I am on assignment," she said slowly. "My first assignment at my first news job in New York. Now how do you think it will look if I become involved with you — the first person I interview in the whole damn city?"

Eric laughed. "As if you're a very attractive — and magnetic — reporter. Which you obviously are. And although I'd rather speak from experience than mere observation, it will look as if a pretty girl I knew seven years ago has grown into a sensuous, interesting woman who doesn't look the other way when something or someone she wants comes along — no matter *who* doesn't like it."

Amanda sighed. "I never said that I was going to let WKM dictate my entire social calendar, Eric."

"But you do want to take it easy."

Amanda nodded. "Yes, exactly," she declared. "I'm glad you finally understand."

Eric nodded. "I suppose I do," he said reluctantly. "Although I can't say I agree or that I'll ever be that way." He sighed. "I've found that much of my life has been spent looking the other way, pretending I didn't want certain things — and certain people — I wanted more than anything in the world," he grated, his voice suddenly rough. "I won't do that anymore, ever again."

Amanda smiled uneasily. His voice had been aggressive and hoarse as he had uttered his last words, as if there were a ruthless streak of ambition in him she had never before glimpsed.

Amanda and Eric fell silent as the taxi pulled up to the entrance of the restaurant. Amanda looked at Eric's dark profile — his brows knit, his jaw set, whether in anger or simply unconsciously she didn't know — and wondered if, in fact, she knew him as well as she had thought. There seemed to be depths of emotions, layers of ambitions, unfulfilled wishes, unspoken oaths of which she was unaware, and she felt suddenly awkward, unsure of herself. Before now she had thought of her renewed acquaintance with Eric as difficult, but a new dimension had been added: It seemed as if something were driving Eric, or distracting him, perhaps — and she had no idea what it was.

But Amanda soon forgot her uncertainties and concerns as she and Eric stepped into the restaurant and out to the outdoor garden section, a breathtakingly beautiful arrangement of white enameled tables and colorful floral bouquets, set against the autumn backdrop of Central Park and the tall buildings nearby.

After they ordered — sole with white grapes in wine sauce, salad, and white wine — Amanda looked at Eric and cleared her throat. "Ahem. Well. I hope you don't mind if I put the tape recorder on the table, Eric. The sound is better that way, and it might trip someone if I put it on the ground." She began fumbling through her purse for the recorder, finally found it, and put it down on the table. Suddenly Eric clapped a strong hand down on hers.

"I do mind," he said roughly.

She looked at him with questions in her eyes, but his eyes reflected only stubborn determination. "Why?" she demanded.

He raised a brow. "I certainly approve of your not putting the damned thing between us, Amanda. I'm not going to have some wire hanging down like that. But I won't have it on anywhere. Not during lunch, in any case."

"But you agreed to give me an interview." She shrugged. "I thought this was going to be a working lunch. I'm much too busy to take this much time for —" It was too dangerous to say "pleasure." "For entertainment."

His eyes penetrated hers with a simmering look that sent a wave of warmth through her that she tried to ignore. "I don't mix business with pleasure, Amanda."

Amanda stared at him, open-mouthed, and then began gathering up her things. "Okay, fine," she said heatedly. "Then I'll just go back to your office and talk to your press aide. You must pay her for precisely this sort of thing." She stood up and slung her purse over her shoulder. "I'll cancel my order through the maître d' on my way out."

Eric reached out and grabbed her wrist. "Just sit down," he growled, "and relax."

Amanda shook her head. "Sorry. You know, Eric, you keep referring to our relationship as if it meant something to you back then —"

"You know it did," he cut in.

Amanda nodded. "Fine. Good. Then let me tell you one reason it meant something to me."

"What was that?" he asked softly, his grip loosening on her wrist.

"Your respect," Amanda said slowly, "was more important to me than you might have imagined, Eric." She closed her eyes and sighed, remembering. When she opened her eyes, Eric gently tugged her wrist so that she sat down again without even realizing it. "*You* know Greg. Or you did then, a bit, and you know how he was — self-absorbed, confused, so involved in his own problems he never even gave my career or aspirations or anything a thought. He considered my work with you a 'diversion' for me, something to keep me busy while he was downtown making deals."

Eric nodded. "I remember."

"And you were the one who encouraged me to try out for some newspaper jobs back then." Amanda laughed. "That almost ended the marriage right then and there." She shook her head. "I wish it had, in a way. It would have been much simpler to end it over simple issues."

Eric slid his hand down and interlaced his fingers with hers, giving her hand a firm squeeze. "We should have been more honest then, Amanda. Both of us."

Amanda withdrew her hand and looked away. "Eric, my marriage couldn't really have ended any sooner. It wouldn't have been right. Greg would have fallen apart."

Eric shrugged. "Maybe not. Sometimes people need to be cut loose to grow, to find out what they're made of." He looked at her intently. "I've thought about all of it a lot, Amanda. We could have managed things very differently." He smiled and shook his head. "And honesty would have been the best place to start." He laughed. "Remember the night before Thanksgiving, when the office had that little party?"

Amanda rolled her eyes. "How could I forget? How late did we stay?"

"It must have been ten or eleven. Everyone else had gone hours earlier."

Amanda met his eyes. "I guess I just hoped one of us would break the rules," she heard herself say.

"And I was hoping the same thing," Eric added, and suddenly his eyes held the promise of what Amanda had been hoping for so fervently that night, hoping for and fearing. As Eric looked at her now, his deep brown eyes drawing her into their depths, she knew he, too, was remembering that night.

At the party they had begun at opposite sides of the room, he with the other attorneys, she with the other paralegals. But they had sent furtive, yet smoldering looks across the room, and then later touched in ways that could have been accidental but weren't, until they both knew they would stay later than the others, to "finish up some business," they told their colleagues . . . and themselves.

But when everyone had gone and they walked together down the quiet hall and stepped into Eric's office, there was a moment when they stood at the doorway in darkness, inches from each other, aware of each breath the other took. Eric finally turned on the light, and the atmosphere was so thick with desire and tension that they suddenly turned away from each other, murmuring words the other couldn't hear. Both were too afraid to reach out and too full of desire to part, too honor-bound to marriage to say "I want you," and too full of emotion to part one moment too soon. They both knew that the choice — the only choice — was either to turn away, or fall into an embrace that would fulfill weeks and months of longing, that would be too strong to stop before it was too late. Before it would perhaps ruin their lives.

Eric smiled sadly and looked thoughtfully at Amanda. "There were hundreds of times I looked back on that night and was sorry . . . that we held back like that."

Amanda looked at him uneasily; she didn't want to discuss it anymore — it was all too dangerous, too uncertain. Thankfully, the waiter appeared with their white wine and broke some of the tension.

"If something had happened between us and you had started it" — he raised an eyebrow — "I suppose I would have felt less guilty." He shook his head. "God, how I wanted you. I must have spent thousands of extra hours at the office because of you." He laughed. "Remember that Forbes project, and how long it took?"

Amanda smiled and rolled her eyes. "I felt

as if we were *married* to that project."

Eric cocked his head. "In a way I guess we both wished we were." He reached out and stroked the back of her hand with his fingertips. "Remember when I lost the Castleton case, and we stayed in my office talking until — what was it? Ten? Eleven?"

Amanda laughed and shook her head. "Eleven thirty. I almost missed the last train out to Connecticut, and Greg nearly went crazy."

As Amanda realized she should withdraw her hand, that Eric's languorous stroking was sending slow waves of warmth through her, as she realized she couldn't meet his deep brown eyes without feeling as if she were being uncontrollably drawn toward him, Eric closed his hand over hers and somehow bade her to look at him, to meet his eyes. And when, unable to stop herself, she looked at him, her lips parted and she succumbed helplessly to warm waves of desire, her eyelids suddenly heavy with longing. "Eric, I —"

"Shh," he whispered, holding up a finger. Then he touched it to her lips. "Don't say anything," he murmured. And he let her go then, taking his finger from her lips and his hand from hers, and she felt suddenly bereft. "That was something we couldn't do in the office," he said, smiling gently. Then his smile broadened into a grin. "One of many possibilities we're now free to . . . explore," and he laughed his rich, deep laugh, his dark eyes flashing with amusement.

She realized her face was flaming and she rolled her eyes. "All right, Eric." She laughed. "It's nice to reminisce and all, but I *would* like to get some interviewing in before it gets too late," she said, looking at her watch and trying to will her cheeks to cool down.

"It's never too late," he said softly.

Amanda sighed. Why was Eric persisting like this? Couldn't he see that she didn't *want* to remember, that the memories created complications and issues she didn't want to confront — not now anyway. She had to bring the discussion back to business. "I'm beginning to think you're reminiscing — talking about memories you may not have even thought of for years, Eric — just to avoid discussing what I'd like to talk about."

He raised a brow. "Politics, for instance?" He smiled sadly. "I certainly remember your feelings about *that*, Amanda." He sighed. "As I recall, politicians are just a step above loan sharks and hit men on your scale."

She nodded and smiled. "Most, yes. Your

memory is accurate. But really, this is all grist for the interview: politics, your ambitions, your plans for the near and distant future."

"All right," he said, eyes gleaming with challenge. "I'll make you a promise. Here's our waiter now. I will *not* discuss any of those fascinating topics you just mentioned while we eat. Filet of sole and politics simply don't mix. But I give you my solemn promise that after lunch I'll be yours." He barely suppressed a smile. "Do with me what you will, Amanda, and you won't hear a word of complaint." He nodded toward the sole as the waiter set the plates on the table. "And please don't mind me if I watch you eat." He winked. "I love to watch a woman when she's really enjoying herself. Although eating is not my first choice of activities."

"Shut up and eat," Amanda muttered, cheeks flaming.

An hour later, as Eric guided Amanda outdoors and down one of the park's prettier paths, Amanda saw he had a smile playing on his lips that sent a wave of apprehension down her spine. "Just what are you up to?" she demanded, as Eric took her arm in his and led her across the road toward the more secluded lakeside paths.

Eric smiled enigmatically and kept walking. "Just come this way," he said quietly, wrapping his arm around her waist. The warmth of his hand through the thin material of her shirt was all she could think about for the moment, as her mind shut out all thoughts other than physical sensations — of his strong hand holding her waist; of his lean thigh brushing against her own; of the slim hips coaxing hers into a gait that was relaxed yet restrained, casual to the detached observer but full of physical meaning to the more primitive centers of Amanda's mind, the senses that said, "Feel this rhythm, this firmness, this tension, this heat, this stride that matches your own as his passion matches your own." For though the embrace was barely an embrace, with Eric's arm simply slung around her waist, it was suddenly as if Amanda's senses had been awakened to the fact that yes, she could have Eric now, she could kiss him and touch him and hold him; she could melt her lips into his, run her mouth along his chest, press her body against him and feel and know and love him; she could moan for him, cry out with him, ache for him, and have her ache satisfied. He was hers if she wanted him. And she wanted him very much.

They stopped walking and she looked around. They were standing in a lovely grove of trees, the sounds of sparrows suddenly more noticeable than the city din Amanda was used to. They watched as a young man walked by with a small white and brown dog, and then they turned to each other, alone at last.

He put his hands on her waist, and she reached up and put her arms around his neck. And then he slowly lowered his mouth to hers, gazing into her eyes until their lips met and they pulled each other close. His lips parted hers and then his warm tongue entwined with her own, and they moaned together over the wonder that it was finally happening — they were finally together after months of desire, years of ache. Eric drew his head back and gazed into her eyes, his dark eyes stormy with longing and pleasure. "I want you," he said huskily, his lips close to hers, his breath warm against her mouth. He lowered his mouth to her neck, and then roved upward to her earlobe, biting it just enough to send a shock of desire through Amanda's veins. She pulled him closer, wanting to feel his lean body against her own, every inch pressing into the softness of her flesh. She felt his desire then and sighed, burying her mouth in his hair, inhaling his warm male scent mixed with the cool autumn air. "Amanda," he murmured, his breath soft and hot in her ear. "Do you feel the way you did then? Do you want me?"

"Yes," she breathed, her eyes closing in passion as he pressed his body against hers. "Yes," she moaned, "I want you."

"Amanda," he breathed, "I can hardly believe I finally have you in my arms."

"Hold me," she murmured, suddenly saddened though she knew not why. He wrapped his arms more tightly around her and held her close, his face nestled in her hair and her head resting against his shoulder.

Then she looked up at him, and he looked down at her, his eyes suddenly filled with doubt. "What's the matter?" he murmured. "You look . . . frightened."

She tried to smile but it came out a half frown, and she shook her head. "I'm sorry," she said, "it's just that everything's happening so fast. I don't see you for seven years, and all of a sudden we seem to be involved in every possible way." She drew her brows together. "I don't even know if you're involved with anyone."

He looked at her steadily. "I'm not," he said quietly.

"But there's so much else I don't know." She pulled away from him a bit. "And I don't want to make a mistake because of . . . because of—"

"Unbridled lust?" he queried, smiling.

"I'm serious," she said, pulling away a bit more. "Eric, it's very difficult to think when I'm in your arms doing something I've wanted to do for a long time."

He sighed and pursed his lips. "What do you suggest?" he asked quietly.

She sighed. "I guess that . . . that we go slowly, and get to know each other again, and see where it leads."

He nodded slowly. "All right," he sighed. "I suppose it makes sense." He shook his head. "But there are ways of getting to know a person, or renewing a friendship, on many levels, Amanda — emotionally, spiritually, physically —"

"I know, Eric," she said evenly. "But I'm talking about myself and my own feelings, and I know what I want. And need."

He nodded again, letting his hands slide reluctantly from her hips. "All right," he repeated, sadness in his eyes.

"And I guess one way we can start is by connecting professionally, with the interviews and all."

His eyes clouded. "I don't think so," he

said slowly, his voice low and wary.

Amanda's eyes widened. "What do you mean, you don't think so?" She gestured at the park. "What about all this? Tavern on the Green, this walk?"

"This walk had nothing to do with an interview, Amanda."

She looked at him in disbelief. "You never had any intentions of giving me an interview, did you?"

He shook his head slowly. "I'm surprised at you, Amanda. Is the interview all you care about?" He frowned. "Seven years ago, had we both been free, we wouldn't have been the slightest bit concerned with things like that at this point."

"Seven years ago, Eric, you didn't make promises and then go back on your word. You didn't play games like this —"

"I don't call the kiss we just shared a 'game,' Amanda. And don't tell me that the only reason you agreed to this lunch was for an interview."

"Of course it wasn't," Amanda said. "Not the only reason. But it's as if you're creating a smoke screen, or trying to — almost as if you're talking about the past just to avoid the present."

"I told you I wanted you off the commission story, Amanda."

"You're not my boss anymore, Eric, and you agreed to give me background information for the close-up, which is separate, in any case." Her eyes flashed at him. "If you continue to try to avoid the interviews, Eric, I don't see how your behavior will really be any different from that of dozens of dishonest political figures I could be speaking with instead."

"Is that what you really think, Amanda? That I'm dishonest?" He gestured into the air. "Just who, then, was the man you spent time with, as you spent time with me, working out all kinds of problems?"

"Maybe you've changed," she said quietly.

"You're hardly very open-minded, Amanda, considering your profession. I can see that you've already made up your mind, that —"

"I haven't," Amanda cut in, "although God knows you haven't given me any reasons to have any confidence in you. You —"

"Wait a minute," Eric interrupted, putting a warm hand on her waist.

"Please take your hand off me, Eric," she breathed. "This is a professional matter, not a personal one."

He stepped forward and put his other hand on her waist, now holding her firmly in his grasp. "Ah, but that's where you're wrong, Amanda. It's a very personal matter. And I imagine you wouldn't say half the things you've just said if I were simply a 'professional contact.' "

Amanda twisted out of his grasp and stepped back, putting enough space between herself and him to lessen the magnetic pull he seemed to exert over her. "All right," she conceded reluctantly. "You're right about that. But are you going to give me some time this afternoon or not?"

He raised a brow. "For the interview?"

"Yes, for the interview!" she snapped.

He held his hands out in a gesture of feigned helplessness. "Amanda, you don't need *me* to give you background information. You *know* me. And as for current questions — about my work on the commission — you know that's off limits."

"I see," she said slowly. "So in other words, the answer is no."

He cocked his head. "How about no with a yes for the future? When my work on the commission is over."

"How about a simple no for good," she seethed, and turned on her heel for the road. "Good-bye, Eric," she called out, and made her way up the path as quickly as she could, her cheeks hot with rage.

Chapter Four

That night Amanda tossed and turned as it grew later and later and she stayed as wide awake as ever. Every time she closed her eyes, she saw Eric's face, felt the warm touch of his hands on her skin, the unrelenting pressure of his lips against her own. And it was not Eric as she had last seen him — angry and selfish — whom she saw now in her tormented wakefulness. No, it was Eric as she cared for him most, laughing with his head back, his dark eyes flashing and hair carelessly falling across his forehead, laughing with that open smile that never lied, that always showed honest, deep enjoyment and amusement and pleasure. She had always loved his smile. She remembered well the first time she had seen that special smile, when she and Eric had been leaving the building for lunch, and a woman was coming through the lobby with a baby in her arms. The baby spotted Eric — for what reason they never fathomed — and let out a delighted cry, reaching for him with both tiny arms. And Eric's eyes lit up and he smiled that broad open smile and gave the baby a pat on the cheek that sent it cooing into another series of delighted cries. And then Eric's expression changed as swiftly as a cloud can shift across the noonday sun, and he had looked unhappy and distracted and tense. Later on, at lunch, he had explained that he and Jillian had had an argument over having children — not their first argument on the subject, and he was certain it would not be their last. He had always wanted children, always assumed it would happen with none of the arguing that somehow always seemed to be a necessary adjunct to everything he and Jillian did. But Jillian had suddenly changed her mind about having children, and there was nothing he could do to change it.

That day at lunch Amanda and Eric had talked the problem through. Eric finally realized that he had been cherishing an idea he had formed before marriage and not really carefully considered since; in fact, he wasn't at all certain Jillian would be a good mother.

Later in the afternoon Eric had thanked Amanda for listening, though he knew as well as she that thanks weren't necessary. And then there was one of those awkward moments they always had, when they each realized they had gotten too close, that once again they were treading on dangerous ground.

Now, as Amanda lay in bed remembering, she wondered what could have happened to change Eric so, to make him so uncaring about her professional needs, so arrogant about his time and what he wanted to do with it. And she realized all at once that there was a totally new aspect to their relationship — in addition to the fact that they were now both free — and that was power, or perhaps ambition. Amanda was now a reporter, with professional needs Eric could satisfy, and at the same time with power of her own that could hurt or help Eric. And Eric was no longer simply a lawyer, with cases that changed from year to year and a staff of loyal and adoring paralegals. Now he was heading up an investigation of critical importance and, more significantly, perhaps running for office. And those were positions that created very different needs for him, with very different parts of his personality coming into dominance. Eric was now someone acutely conscious of people's opinions and thoughts, someone acutely conscious of the media. And Amanda *was* the media.

Didn't he, then, realize that her story on

him was of major importance? And didn't he care about its importance in *her* career, as her first assignment at her first job in New York?

She had gotten absolutely no information from him so far, other than what every other reporter who had bothered to come to the press conference had. And in a little more than a week WKM was planning to broadcast the close-up, which meant that Amanda had only one option open: She would have to go ahead and pursue the commission story *and* information about Eric — perhaps with the help of Sheila Farnham, Eric's press aide — without Eric's cooperation. She was not going to lose her job or perform poorly because of him, no matter what she had to do to succeed.

Amanda turned toward the window and looked out at the few windows still lit in the building across the street. At least she wasn't the only person still awake. Was Eric tossing and turning, too? She could imagine him now as she had seen him at home once seven years ago, though he had lived in a different apartment then. He had sent for her when he was home with a newly broken ankle and needed some papers. It was the first time she had ever been at his apartment, and, not having met Jillian before, she was nervous about meeting her. Was Jillian as jealous as Greg of the relationship Eric and Amanda shared?

But Jillian wasn't home, and Eric had answered the door himself, wearing only blue silk pajamas and worn-out leather slippers. Amanda had blushed wildly the minute he had opened the door — the finely cut silk showed every detail of his masculine frame, from his bulky shoulders to his narrow hips to his strong hard thighs, and Amanda was overwhelmed by the closeness of him.

He hadn't shaved, and his face looked pleasantly rough, as if its touch would send pleasurable pulses of not-quite pain as it brushed against her skin, as she rubbed her cheek against his, her neck against his neck, against the fine hairs covering his warm chest. "Anything wrong?" he had asked, and her cheeks had flamed deeper still as she looked away quickly. But when she began to hand him the papers, she was so distracted that she dropped them and quickly stooped to pick them up. And she looked at him again from the floor as she began gathering up what she had dropped — her eyes taking in the muscular male hips in that thin material and, where the bottoms and the top met, a thin line of black hair going down the middle of his flat stomach. The blue silk looked somehow more fragile against his obviously powerful frame of pure muscle and force.

He had bent down then, too, to help her, and when he looked up and began to say "I'm sor—" he fell silent as his dark eyes penetrated hers and told her he felt as she did, that he wanted to take her in his arms and join together in a powerful, thrusting union they'd neither one ever forget.

And they had both stuttered and stammered through the rest of the visit, until it was time for Amanda to go — early because they weren't accomplishing what they had planned in the way of work.

Amanda turned over, put the pillow over her head, and tried to think of something — anything — other than Eric. Of course, tomorrow she'd have to spend the whole day concentrating on him. But with any luck she wouldn't see him for a good long time — and maybe then he would have realized how selfish he was being.

The next morning Amanda could hardly drag herself out of bed and in to work. After having gotten only three hours' sleep, she looked far from her best, with her usually pale skin paler still and her normally bright eyes dull with fatigue. She had pulled her auburn hair into a passably neat ponytail and put on enough gray eye shadow to make her eyes look darker than the circles under them, but she knew no amount of makeup was going to make her look as good as she could. But what did it matter, anyway? Whom was she trying to impress?

But at least she was wearing a new outfit she had splurged on — a navy and white silk shirt and navy gabardine pants, which she had bought in white, too, because they fit so smoothly over her slim hips.

Once in the office, Amanda set to work right away, shutting the glass door to her cubicle and laying out an enormous pile of index cards in front of her. She'd outline what she knew about Eric professionally, what she needed to know for the close-up, and theories she had about the direction in which the commission was headed. This information could then guide her in her interviews with whomever would speak with her.

Seeing that she needed some background information about licensing practices, she dialed Greg for some help. Using him for assistance wasn't an entirely satisfactory course of action to her — enlisting his help was something he'd grasp at and hang on to for weeks, probably calling her every other day with more information than she had ever wanted, and then referring to the incident for months afterward. But she did need the information, and Greg was the simplest source on whom to call.

As she had predicted, he was happy to hear from her, and initially overeager to supply her with information on general practices. But when Amanda mentioned the commission's investigation and asked what specifically Eric had wanted from Greg, he became evasive and, stranger still for him, almost curt.

"Amanda, you'll never know all you have to know for this story. The background's too complicated. Give it to one of the real-estate guys at the station."

"We don't have any 'real-estate guys,' or women, at the station, Greg."

There was a silence, then: "I'm sorry to hear that, Amanda. I've got to go." And he hung up after a very quick good-bye.

Greg's behavior was as uncharacteristic as Amanda had ever seen; something was wrong, and it had to be directly connected with Eric in some way, as Greg had become evasive only when the commission had come up. Could it be, Amanda wondered, that Eric was investigating business dealings directly traceable to Greg? Could Greg be in trouble, or at least under suspicion?

On that hunch Amanda picked up the phone and dialed Eric's office, hoping Eric wouldn't answer; she was planning to disguise her voice, which she hadn't done in years, and had no idea how it would come out. When an unfamiliar voice answered, Amanda asked for Sheila Farnham. And when Sheila picked up, Amanda said in a painfully low voice that she was Greg Warner's secretary, and that Greg was interested in meeting with Mr. Harrison.

And she hit pay dirt. Sheila couldn't disguise the excitement in her voice as she said, "Mr. Harrison will be very pleased to hear that. How would two o'clock this afternoon be?"

"Fine," Amanda answered, said goodbye, and hung up. She was excited over the fact that she had discovered something significant — namely, that Eric's investigation did indeed involve Greg in some way — but she was equally apprehensive, even horrified. What had Greg done? And she was also a bit concerned that she had done something dishonest at best and professionally suicidal at worst. Certainly the simple ruse she was performing was minor compared to some of the tricks investigative reporters routinely resorted to. But she wasn't supposed to be an investigative reporter, and presumably kept as aboveboard as possible in her research and coverage. But she had learned something, dishonestly or not — and chances were good that she would learn more still if she arrived at Eric's office at the appointed time and confronted him with her bits and pieces of knowledge.

As the time drew near for Amanda to leave for Eric's office, she realized she was more nervous than she had expected to be. What would Eric say when he saw her in Greg's place? He would have every right to be furious, accusing her of the very dishonesty she had confronted him with the day before.

And the fact that she neither looked nor felt her best didn't help matters one bit. She went into the bathroom and put on some cinnamon-toned lipstick that brought out the highlights of her hair, and touched up her mascara and eyeliner a bit, but she still looked like exactly what she was: an exhausted young woman who had had exactly three hours of sleep. Well, she wasn't entering a beauty contest anyway; she was confronting a former acquaintance in order to force a story, to force him to let her in on whatever he was doing so that she could do well on her first assignment. And she didn't need to look her best to do that, did she?

When Amanda arrived at Eric's office building at the appointed time, she paced the lobby a few times to let some time pass. She wanted to be sure Eric would be ready in his office; otherwise, the shock value of the entire stunt would be lost. Then she pressed her way into a crowded postlunch elevator, got out at Eric's floor, took several deep breaths, and opened the door to the commission headquarters.

It was as busy as ever, with young people running this way and that carrying sheafs of papers, calling to each other and talking busily on the phone, typing away at lightning speed. Amanda unconsciously set aside her criticisms of Eric at that moment as she was once again impressed with his operation: the frenzied industriousness of all the staff members indicated an obvious respect for Eric on the part of all the people who worked for him.

Amanda threaded her way through the crowded aisles between the desks. When she reached Sheila's vacant desk outside Eric's office, the door suddenly flew open and Amanda turned.

Eric was standing there, stock still, pale as a sheet as he stared at her.

"What in hell are you doing here?" he rasped. A thick lock of dark hair hung down over his forehead, and he angrily pushed it back. His shirt sleeves were rolled up, exposing thick forearms covered with dark curling hairs. As usual, he wore no tie, and his pale blue shirt was partially unbuttoned. "Well?" he demanded roughly.

Amanda swallowed, took a deep breath, and spoke. "I'm here instead of Greg," she said calmly.

And then his face darkened, and his eyes clouded in anger. "What?" he demanded.

"I said, I'm here instead of Greg," she repeated. "Greg isn't coming."

Eric turned on his heel and stormed into his office, then gestured angrily for her to follow. She did, though she wasn't certain it was a good idea.

He shut the door and turned to face her, in a wrathful pose that left her knees weak. "Now, explain yourself. I don't have the slightest idea what you're talking about."

Something in his irritated tone allowed her to draw courage — he had no right to be so nasty — and Amanda drew herself up to her full height, tilting up her chin in anger. "What I'm talking about," she said steadily, "is Greg, my ex-husband, whom you've been so cryptic about lately. I decided that there was something odd going on when I spoke with Greg this morning and he became unusually reticent after I mentioned your name."

"Go on," Eric grated, his voice hoarse with anger. He turned and walked over to his desk and sat against the edge of it, extending his long legs forward and crossing his thick arms. He looked more relaxed than before, but Amanda suspected that his relaxation was more feigned than genuine, merely designed to throw her off guard. His eyes still flashed with anger, and his hard jaw was clenched.

"Well," Amanda began, walking casually past Eric toward the bookcase; somehow she felt more comfortable pacing. "I knew there was something odd going on between you and Greg, as I said —"

"Stop that," he interrupted gruffly.

"Stop what?" she flared, raising a brow in irritation.

Eric's eyes darkened. "How do you expect me to listen to your story when you're parading back and forth like that?" he demanded. "My God, Amanda, if those pants were any tighter I'd think they were sprayed on."

Amanda's cheeks flamed as she narrowed her eyes at Eric. "I'd hardly call these tight," she blazed. "And stop trying to distract me, dammit!"

His lips curved in amusement. "That's funny; I was just about to ask the same of you."

"Never mind," she muttered, turning away, sorry she had said anything and sorrier still when she faced Eric again and saw that he was still just barely suppressing a mocking smile.

"All right," he said. "Go on, Amanda. I'm waiting."

"Okay," she said in as flip a manner as she could manage. "Sensing what I did about you and Greg, and after Greg wouldn't tell me anything, I knew the only way I'd get to you would be to pull something like this. For one thing, you'd have to see me —"

"I'm always ready to see you," he cut in, looking at her with hooded dark eyes.

"I mean on the story, Eric," she said stiffly. "And I felt you'd probably decide it would be better to let me in on the story than to let me have the scraps I have now. You know, bits of information in a reporter's hands can be dangerous," she said daringly. "It would be better if you spilled the whole thing, Eric."

"Oh, would it?" he rasped. "Why I ought to . . ."

Her brows lifted in surprised amusement. "Ought to what?" she dared, planting her

107

hands on her waist.

And suddenly he pushed himself off the desk and was striding toward her, a gleam in his eye that Amanda could not recall having seen before. Whether out of courage, or fear, she stood her ground, meeting his gaze boldly.

In two long strides he had reached her and caught her wrists in his hands. "I was wrong when I said you hadn't changed," he said huskily, holding her imprisoned wrists tightly in his. "You've gotten quite tough, lady, haven't you?" He pursed his lips and grinned. "I think I like this new Amanda even better," he said speculatively, letting her hands go.

"And maybe we should both drop the theatrics, Eric," she replied, ignoring the pounding of her heart. "I won't pretend to be Greg's secretary or anyone I'm not, and you'll stop overplaying the role of 'important new politician in the midst of a confidential investigation.' In other words, we can cooperate with each other as old friends and stop all of this underhandedness" — she raised an eyebrow — "my latest actions included. I honestly would have preferred another way."

Eric shook his head and walked over to his desk. "One moment," he said to Amanda, and then buzzed the intercom and picked up the receiver. "Sheila, yes. Uh, Greg Warner won't be coming in after all, so you can send back all the equipment . . . Yes . . . No, it was a mix-up, that's all. Talk to you later."

When he hung up, he looked at Amanda and slowly shook his head. "If it had been anyone else, Amanda —" Anger flared in his eyes. "If anyone else had dared to pull a stunt like this, I would have done my best to have him or her kicked off the assignment and out of broadcasting — for as long as possible if not forever."

Amanda raised a brow. "Isn't that just a bit dictatorial, Eric? Reporters have to do whatever they can to get a story. What about the proverbial 'people's right to know'?"

"That right to know is curtailed and sometimes eliminated when it has the potential to jeopardize a serious investigation," he said gruffly, coming around to the front of the desk and leaning against it. "And this business I'm involved in is serious, Amanda. It involves people who, through bribery and greed and dishonesty, are literally endangering the lives of thousands of people every day. Which means that I have to operate under conditions of the utmost secrecy."

Amanda sighed and looked into Eric's

eyes. "Look. I'm sorry, but you didn't make it easy for me, Eric, and I have a job to do. You didn't have to ask me to give up the story, you know. You put me in a very awkward position. Put yourself in my place: How would it have looked if you had turned down your first case at the firm, and when one of the senior partners asked why, you had said, 'Well, the opponent asked me to'?"

"It's hardly analogous, Amanda. But I admit I see part of your point. I think you're right that we might as well both come clean." He paused. "None of this would have happened if I had done that at the beginning."

He walked over to her then, slowly, his eyes never leaving hers. He reached out and gently brushed a strand of her hair back from her forehead, and then lifted her chin with a forefinger. "But it's very difficult," he said softly, "when I'm distracted by eyes I've thought about for seven years, Amanda. Since I saw you at the press conference, I've done nothing as I had planned." His eyes clouded. "But we could hardly have met under worse circumstances, Amanda."

"What do you mean?" she asked quietly.

His jaw tensed and he closed his eyes. When he opened them, they were deep with regret. "I'm investigating Greg, Amanda." He shook his head. "It wasn't definite — I thought we might be wrong. But we were right. And we're going ahead. I'm sorry."

Amanda frowned. "But what does that mean, exactly? What has he done?"

Eric sighed. "Look. It — I think it would be better if we talked in a more private place. Where we could really talk," he said gravely.

"Eric, you're making it sound very serious."

"It *is* serious, Amanda," he said solemnly. "Look, I don't really have a free moment between now and Friday — things are moving very quickly — but I can make time for you tonight. It's important."

Amanda bit her lip. There was a staff meeting at WKM that was supposed to go until nine or ten. "What about after ten, Eric? We have a staff meeting, and —"

"Fine," he cut in. "I can get in some extra work, then. Give me a call when your meeting's over, and I'll come pick you up. We can have coffee at my place."

Amanda looked up sharply. "I didn't think —"

"Amanda," Eric said, grasping her shoulders, "it's absolutely crucial that we talk privately. My place or yours — it doesn't make a bit of difference to me. Just not a restaurant where we could possibly be overheard."

She swallowed. "Okay," she said uncertainly. "Your place, then."

"Then I'll expect to hear from you later," Eric said, suddenly bending down and kissing her lightly on the mouth. "Now get out of here before I change my mind."

"Right," Amanda murmured, and she drifted out in a daze, a thousand thoughts crowding her mind.

And, somehow voicing itself more loudly than any of the other thoughts, what would happen at Eric's apartment?

Chapter Five

Amanda could barely concentrate on her work for the rest of the day after meeting with Eric. Her feelings and moods coalesced and shifted as bits of conversations came into her mind and then faded away, and she felt as if her mind were inexorably fated to travel in circles of indecision forever. What had Greg done? Though respect or any real feeling for Greg had long ago died, Amanda felt the vestiges of concern for him, for the man she had once called her husband.

And Eric — he had at once been gallant and condescending, caring and unthinking: for in trying to protect her from involvement in a story that could hurt her and possibly damage her credibility at WKM, he had assumed — consciously or unconsciously — that she was incapable of dealing with the situation maturely and professionally. And as it had turned out, neither he nor she had done very well so far: he had been cryptic, vague, and almost dishonest, and she had resorted to trickery in an attempt to force him to tell the truth. At least now they were going to deal with each other honestly.

But how well could she trust him? He had been less than honest with her personally as well as professionally, at one moment telling her he didn't want to see her, at the next moment kissing her passionately. They seemed to be communicating even less now than they had seven years ago, when they had been limited by outside forces and issues rather than by inner feelings and motives.

And Eric was not the only one to blame. She was as guilty as he, more willing to resort to game-playing and subterfuge than to speak honestly, not just about the problem with the commission story but about the relationship as well. She knew that the attraction between herself and Eric was stronger than ever, but beyond that she was afraid to look.

Later, during the staff meeting, at one point Amanda was so deeply involved in her thoughts about Eric that she didn't even realize Stan had asked her a question. She was suddenly aware of a silence, and then a sharp pain as Vivian kicked her under the table. All she could do was look at Stan questioningly and say "I'm sorry — ?" And he gave her a black look, muttered, "Never mind," and asked somebody else what he thought.

Amanda was alert for the remainder of the meeting; it simply wouldn't do to appear inattentive on top of all the other problems she would perhaps have to reveal to Stan in the next few weeks if she couldn't pursue her interviews with Eric.

When the meeting was over, Amanda was about to dash out of the room to pull herself together in the ladies' room before calling Eric, when Stan called her over and asked her to come into his office.

When they were inside, he closed the door and sat down behind his desk. "What's wrong?" he asked bluntly.

"What?"

He shrugged. "What's wrong? You didn't hear one word that was exchanged in that meeting tonight."

Amanda shook her head. "I'm sorry, Stan. I'm very tired."

He nodded slowly. "Working hard?"

"Yes, yes," she said quickly.

"Story on Harrison coming along okay?"

"Yes, fine."

He sighed and leaned forward. "Look, Amanda, occasionally I run into problems here at the station, especially with new reporters. You see, I'm a nice guy and everyone knows it." He looked at her steadily. "But I'm a nice *guy*, Amanda. Not necessarily a nice boss. I expect work to get done around here, and I expect it to get done right and on time. And if that isn't going to happen, I want to know about it. In advance. *Well* in advance."

Amanda nodded, silent.

He put his palms on the desk and stood up. "As long as you understand, Amanda. I want to know when something isn't going right. And that means the second it happens."

"I understand," Amanda said quietly.

Stan looked at her carefully and then turned away. "All right, see you tomorrow," he said.

As Amanda left his office, she couldn't help wondering whether she had imagined a certain sadness in Stan's voice. Did he know things weren't going right with the story on Eric? If Eric didn't agree tonight to go ahead with all aspects of both stories — on himself and the commission — Amanda had an obligation to let Stan know right away. As things stood now, Stan seemed to be bending over backward in her favor, and he deserved to be told the truth.

Amanda hurried down the hall toward the ladies' room, looking at her watch as she ran. Damn! It was already ten. Eric hated to be kept waiting for anyone or anything, and his temper would probably be starting to fray at the edges by now.

"Oh!" Amanda cried as she bumped into someone. "I'm —"

It was Eric. Smiling, he grasped her by the shoulders and said, "Hey, slow down. Where are you running off to?"

He looked tired but wonderful, his face dark and unshaven and his hair carelessly mussed. And although in the cool autumn evenings most men were wearing trench coats, Eric wore only a light tweed jacket.

Amanda smiled. "Just the ladies' room, Eric. I was going to call you in a few minutes."

He raised a brow. "Well, I'm glad of that. I was beginning to wonder."

She shot him a mock-angry look. "You're the one who was trying to avoid *me*, Eric, remember?"

He didn't smile; he only looked into her eyes with a deep regret that nearly brought tears to her eyes. Although he had known she was joking, he was obviously sorry as well. "I wish we could start all over again," he said quietly, something in his voice making her knees begin to go weak. "I *am* sorry, Amanda."

Amanda blinked back the wetness in her eyes and smiled. "We can start over again tonight," she said.

"I'm glad," he said softly, and squeezed her shoulders. "I'll meet you down the hall."

"Okay," Amanda said, and turned down the corridor for the ladies' room. A few minutes later, having brushed her hair and washed her face, Amanda made her way back down the hallway to meet Eric; but her heart skipped a beat when she saw Eric in Stan's office, his head bowed and his hands clasped together in seriousness. Stan looked solemn, too, his heavy face thinned by a frown, darkened by thick brows pulled closely together. Damn Eric! Why had he gone in to see Stan, when he had to know his being there would lead to questions about what sort of relationship he and Amanda had. After all, it was late at night, and he was there to pick Amanda up. And what were Stan and Eric being so serious about? Perhaps Stan had discovered that Amanda had made virtually no headway on the stories whatsoever. She shook her head, wishing she had been honest with Stan, but her actions as well as her thoughts and feelings had been muddled since she had first seen Eric again.

When Stan signaled through the glass for Amanda to come in, she knew all at once that he hadn't learnt some terrible piece of news about her, that they probably hadn't even been discussing her. He was smiling broadly, a man who had gotten together with an old poker buddy for a few minutes.

"Hey, Amanda," Stan cried as she came in, "you didn't tell me how close Eric has come to the nomination."

"I —"

"I've asked Amanda to keep a lid on it," Eric cut in. "Things are so indefinite right now that the wrong person hearing the wrong word could tip the scales the other way."

"I understand," Stan said, waving a hand of dismissal. "But if it goes too far, Eric, we've got to break the story." He turned to Amanda. "Which I'm sure Amanda will warn me about."

She forced a smile. "Of course."

Later, as Amanda and Eric walked wordlessly down the street toward the corner, Amanda turned to Eric and broke the silence. "Eric, I wish you hadn't gone in to see Stan." She sighed. "My situation is complicated enough as it is without having people gossip about me as well. Half the copy girls and typists in the room completely stopped working to stare at you."

He smiled. "I'm glad *someone* has good taste."

Amanda didn't smile. "Eric, I'm serious. You have to remember that I'm new at WKM — you're my first assignment — and I'd look really bad professionally if people started talking, which they will. I haven't established myself in any way yet, and I can't afford to have any little slipups or indiscretions — any."

Eric stopped and gently turned her to face him. "Amanda, I promise you have nothing to worry about. I made sure of that."

"Oh, did you?" she snapped. "And what makes you think I want you making my decisions for me, or trying to protect me?" She shook her head. "Stan gave me a warning tonight — one of the nicest I've ever received, but it was still a warning, Eric. Because he already suspects I'm not doing the bang-up job he had expected."

Eric shook his head and then slowly leaned forward and lightly brushed his lips against hers. "Don't worry," he murmured. "I'll take care of everything," he breathed softly, gently grazing his lips along her cheek to her ear. "I promise. I want to help, Amanda. That's what friends are for," he whispered, and the gentle touch of his breath in her hair and the woodsy, male scent that was uniquely his own, the roughness of his cheek, and the deep muskiness she inhaled from his dark hair made her want to wrap her arms around him and hold him close, claim his mouth with hers and open her lips to his searching tongue, to . . . But she knew she couldn't and murmured, "No," and pushed Eric back. She turned away and crossed her arms, suddenly feeling chilled, as if a great blanket of warmth had just been whisked away from her.

Then she felt warm strong hands on her shoulders, and she forced herself to step forward out of their grasp once again. "Amanda," Eric said quietly.

"No," she answered, turning around. His eyes were searching, deep, questioning, tender, but Amanda forced herself to go on with what she had intended to say. "Eric, we can't talk seriously about the commission or anything else if —"

"If we make love?" he interrupted softly.

Amanda's heart skipped a beat. "Not just that," she began.

He raised a brow. "In other words, 'hands off' for a while. Is that what you're saying?"

Amanda tried to hush the inner voice that was protesting from somewhere deep inside. "Yes," she said. And then heard herself say, "For now, at least."

Eric pursed his lips and looked at her

thoughtfully. "For now," he repeated, nodding. "Now let's grab a cab and get all of this serious talking over with." His eyes gleamed. "You don't mind if I take your arm while we look for a cab, do you? It's only proper and safe on the streets of New York."

Amanda smiled. "Of course not."

And as they walked arm in arm, she on the left, he on the right, they walked in step, as if they did this all the time, as if, too, their bodies had been made for each other. Amanda tried to ignore her feelings when her hip brushed against his, when he pressed her arm more tightly against him, when their eyes met in a look of desire that was broken — out of apprehension — as spontaneously as it had been created. For even though she had made certain resolves, and expressed certain reservations to Eric, there was no way she could keep her senses from reacting; it was as if, despite Amanda's mind, her body knew that the seven-year wait was over, and the lean, strong man only inches away was ready, willing, and eager to be close to her, to be part of her life.

The taxi ride over to Eric's was filled with tension. Eric was silent, clenching his jaw and occasionally looking out the window, and Amanda let her futile attempt at light conversation die after she realized how silly it was to try to fill up a silence with Eric. There was no point in pretending the mood wasn't tense with anticipation, heavy with a variety of expectations on both their parts that would or perhaps wouldn't come to fruition. And the thickest tension of all was tinged with a bit of sadness, as Amanda realized with regret that tonight, the first time she was going to Eric's new apartment — a scenario that had been part of her daydreams for years — she had asked him not even to touch her. But she had to admit that, despite some regret, she was glad she had voiced her wishes, for they had serious matters to discuss. Most important of all, her judgment — about Eric as well as professional problems — completely disappeared at Eric's lightest touch, whether it was a finger grazing her cheek or lips brushed lightly against hers, the pressure of his thigh or the sandy feel of his cheek against hers. Even now, though they weren't touching at all, though all was silent except for the sounds of the city and the faint melodies coming from the driver's radio, Amanda's senses were aroused simply by Eric's nearness, almost as if Eric were holding her in his arms.

When the cab pulled up in front of a small

stone house on Riverside Drive and Seventy-seventh Street, Amanda turned to Eric in amazement. "You live in that little building?" she cried. "My God, I love this building. I pass it every day on the bus on my way to work. I thought you lived in one of the big buildings down the block."

He shook his head as he paid the driver. "Uh-uh, not for me, Amanda. I had enough years living in a modern high rise to last a lifetime. Now I have a fireplace and brick walls and ceilings you don't have to stoop under, and it suits me just fine."

Amanda smiled. It was so like Eric to have found the perfect apartment for himself, even in a city where it was nearly impossible to rent the tiniest closet at a price you could afford.

And his apartment, facing Riverside Park from the third story, was more charming than she had even expected, with high oak-beamed ceilings, hand-woven Navaho rugs draped over comfortable-looking low-slung couches and chairs, and a country-style kitchen area at the far end of the living room.

Amanda turned to Eric. "I don't see the fireplace," she said.

He smiled mysteriously. "That, my darling Amanda, is because it's in the bedroom." He raised an eyebrow. "Come. We'll light a fire together." Amanda's cheeks flamed. He gestured for her to precede him through an oak-beamed archway, and Amanda turned quickly so he wouldn't see her high color. He was just barely managing to quell a smile she knew she'd prefer not to see.

Amanda walked down a short hallway and then stood in a darkened doorway, with the lights of New Jersey glimmering on the river right outside the leaded casement windows. Eric came up behind her and flicked on the light, and Amanda was once again reminded of that night in the office those seven years ago, when she and Eric had stood together in the darkness, each wondering whether the other would take the first step, hoping yet fearing that it would happen, that they would fall into each other's arms, melt into each other until it would be too late to stop.

"Well?" Eric prodded quietly. And then Amanda looked at the room and smiled. It was lovely, as cozy-looking as the living room, with Navaho blankets on the bed and hangings on the walls; around the fireplace there were large woven cushions, and a fur rug with two low coffee tables to either side of the fireplace. "Oh, Eric, it's lovely," Amanda cried, turning around to face him.

But she hadn't expected him still to be standing so close, and she inhaled her breath sharply as Eric leaned down and covered her lips with his own. He wrapped his arms around her and moaned as he held her close, running his hands along her back and pressing his hips against hers. She wrapped her arms around his neck, her body coursing with a sudden warmth like hot liquid running through her veins, every inch of her aroused and receptive and wanting more. His lips parted hers and she welcomed his searching tongue into her mouth, its warm wet tip gently thrusting and probing as Amanda felt herself softening, weakening, wanting to open and give herself up to Eric and the desire so quickly ignited between them. Her soft, yielding body bore upon his with greater urgency; he pressed even closer, and she felt the strength of his male need against her.

"Amanda," Eric groaned, his lips grazing her mouth, then her neck. She buried her face in his hair and inhaled his woodsy scent. And then his lips claimed hers and parted them again, and she arched her body so that she could feel every inch of his masculine desire. "Amanda," he rasped hoarsely, "I want you so much."

Amanda closed her eyes and let her head

fall back as Eric kissed the smooth skin of her neck, his lips wet and warm and tender. "Come," he murmured, drawing his head back and exerting a gentle pressure on her shoulder, leading her toward the bed. Ignoring a tiny inner voice of protest, Amanda opened her eyes and gazed at Eric, at the dark heavy-lidded eyes stormy with hunger, and, wordlessly, walked with him.

His eyes never leaving hers, he gently guided her down, so that she sat at the edge of the bed looking up at him, his bulky frame towering over her. Her eyes roved over his tall form — his massive chest, expanding and contracting in desire, his narrow hips encircled by a thick leather belt, his muscular thighs.

"After seven years," he said hoarsely, "I look at you — those teasing eyes, those lips that have silently promised to kiss me everywhere." He inhaled deeply. "And I can't believe we're finally together." He lowered himself to the bed and then guided her back, his strong body easing over hers and his warm hands covering her shoulders. He leaned down and covered her mouth with his gently, then drew his head back and looked into her eyes. "Look at me," he demanded hoarsely, and she opened her eyes, hazy with yearning. His liquid eyes were hypnotic, and she looked at them through a heated fog of hunger, of surging warmth radiating through her body, and begged with her eyes for more. "Do you feel as you did then, Amanda?" he groaned hoarsely, his lips close to hers.

"Yes," she moaned, feeling the urgency of his need. "Yes, Eric. Please."

"I want to see you," he murmured, his face dark with passion, and his fingers set to work, rapidly unbuttoning her shirt. She squirmed as he worked, wanting him to hurry, and gripped his shoulders as he smoothed open her shirt and inhaled deeply, his eyes half closing under dark lashes.

Gently but firmly, he placed his rough palm over her breast and caressed her. "You're so lovely," he murmured. Amanda cried out and reached for him, wanting his mouth — on her lips, on her neck, on her breasts, anywhere, and with a hoarse groan of desire he lowered his head and slid down along her body, trailing his wet mouth from her neck to the rise of her breasts, to a hardened nipple tingling with pleasure. Amanda buried her face in the dark tangle of his hair, tugging at it with frenzied hands and moaning with yearning.

He slid a hand along the side of her body,

and then gently stroked her legs, kneading her sensitive inner thigh in urgent grasping circles. "Eric," she moaned, as his hand found its way to the waistband of her pants and began working at the fastener. She felt the tightness of her pants ease as his fingers undid the fastener, and then his hand tormentingly moved on, tracing hot circles up to her bare midriff, down her thigh, and back again as he expertly coaxed and probed, setting Amanda's senses in a spiraling heat she had never known.

She clutched at his hair and welcomed the heaviness of his body as he once again laid his length along her. He rubbed his sandpapery cheek against hers and took her earlobe in his hot mouth, biting it gently and then letting go, his breath hot and awakening her body to the ever-increasing urgency of her desire. "Eric," she breathed.

"Shh," he whispered. But her need was too great now, and her body writhed beneath him, coaxing, urging, as her hands raked along his back. "Eric, I want you," she moaned into the thick tangle of his hair.

And then the movements of his body slowed, and stopped. Eric drew his head back, and looked into Amanda's questioning eyes with liquid eyes dark with desire. "We can't do this," he said hoarsely, and he closed his eyes and laid his head next to hers, his face damp and rough against the smooth skin of her cheek.

"I don't understand," she said quietly, her voice still thick with desire, her body still crying out for more.

He sighed and raised his head again, and looked into her eyes. "It's —" He shook his head then. "My God, I deserve a medal for this." He inhaled deeply. "But it's wrong."

"What are you talking about?" Amanda cried. "We're here *now,* Eric. This isn't seven years ago. We're free!" The passion in her voice shocked her.

He breathed deeply, and a drop of sweat fell onto one of Amanda's bare breasts. "Amanda, we're not ready. It can't happen yet. I don't want to lose you again, dammit, and I know you." His lips were a tight, grim line. "I haven't forgotten what you said yesterday."

She narrowed her eyes. "You mean about waiting?" she whispered. She felt her breath slowing now, her heart beginning to return to normal. "But that was . . ." Her voice trailed off.

"That was only yesterday, Amanda," he said softly. "Look, I'm not interested in a one-night stand. If sex were all that was important, believe me I could have more than enough. I want *you*," he murmured, "and I know you meant what you said yesterday." He sighed. "And I'm not even sure that *I'm* ready." He paused and shook his head. "I don't want to ever . . . *ever* regret anything that happens between the two of us. Do you understand?"

Amanda closed her eyes. "I suppose you're right," she said. "It's one thing to want you when we're . . . together like this, and another to think about it afterward." She sighed. "I guess I do need more time. Making love with you now would be as important in terms of implications as it would have been then, seven years ago."

"For me, too," he said quietly. "For me, too, Amanda." He sighed. "Well, look, why don't we get out of this chamber of temptation and have some coffee. Unless you'd prefer some wine — ?"

Amanda smiled and shook her head. "I think we'd better stick with coffee tonight."

He smiled. "Right," he agreed, and eased himself to Amanda's side and sat up. He turned to her and shook his head and began gently buttoning her blouse. "Not something I particularly want to do," he muttered.

He finished, and they looked at each other wordlessly, with frustration and acquies-

131

cence, acceptance and regret, passing between them as they contemplated what they had done, and what they had forsaken. Slowly, they stood and walked out of the bedroom, through the living room to the kitchen area.

As Eric prepared the coffee, Amanda sat on one of the two high stools in the breakfast nook, facing the Hudson and the sparkling skyscrapers beyond. She knew now that Eric had been right, much as she had wanted their lovemaking to go on. There was still so much she needed to know about him — both to rediscover and to learn for the first time — and she was glad they had stopped when they had.

Eric set the cups out on a tray and looked at Amanda, his eyes growing apprehensive and thoughtful. "I wish we had talked first," he said quietly. "Before we began to make love. I . . . we'll see . . ." he trailed off, sighing.

Amanda was tempted to tell him not to worry about what he'd be telling her about Greg. She had succeeded in separating herself from Greg's problems and from Greg. But she kept her feelings to herself as Eric lifted the tray and suggested they go into the living room.

A few moments later, as she sat listening

to the apparently endless list of criminal types Greg was suspected of being involved with, Amanda was stunned. But, after all, not surprised. Greg was a man of weak character, a fact she had known for years. No, it was truly not surprising to her that he had gotten himself involved in such shady dealings. She felt for him now the only emotion she had been able to feel in response to him for years — a pitying sadness.

Eric, sitting next to Amanda on the couch, looked down at his steepled fingers. "Amanda, it's really very serious. As my informants have it laid out, Greg is the middleman for a whole series of corrupt officials. When someone wants to, say, open a restaurant without the necessary fire-escape routes, the money — a payoff — goes through Greg to the buildings inspection branch of the fire department. If the guy wants to hire a friend of his who isn't legally allowed to work in the restaurant, the guy will make a payoff to the State Liquor Authority — again, through Greg. If he —"

"Stop," Amanda implored. "Please stop, just for a moment." Tears were beginning to well up and she simply couldn't stand to hear any more. The man Eric was talking about was a man she had once loved, and though what she felt for him now was made

up more of pity than concern, more of sentiment than deep caring, it was all still somewhat painful to hear. She turned to Eric and
narrowed her eyes at him. "Just what led
you to suspect Greg, anyway? What makes
you so sure you're right?"

Eric shook his head. "I didn't say we *were*
sure, Amanda. Which is one reason the investigation is strictly confidential and extremely delicate at this point, and one
reason I didn't want you to know about it. If
it turned out Greg was innocent, it would
have been unnecessary ever to tell you."

Amanda widened her eyes. "I can't believe what I'm hearing, Eric. You're talking
like a lawyer now, or a politician," she said
sadly. "What do you mean, it would have
been unnecessary to tell me? I thought we
were going to be honest with each other."

"And that's what we're doing," Eric
stated. "And you're misunderstanding me. I
didn't want to lie to you, Amanda. But it was
a choice between hurting you unnecessarily
and lying, and I chose the latter."

Amanda was silent. She could hardly believe this was Eric speaking, the Eric she had
respected so highly years ago, the Eric who
had held integrity up as one of the most important virtues a human being can possess.
"I don't like to hear you say things like that,

Eric. It doesn't sound like you."

"I was trying to protect you, Amanda," he declared. "I didn't *want* to lie — or to hide the truth."

"Ah. Another politician's distinction from the new Eric Harrison, with his politician's dictionary of terms," she said sarcastically. She hated the way she sounded — the biting quality of her voice made her want to cry — but she went on. "I think I could do with a little less protection, Eric. First you 'hide the truth' from me without explaining anything, so I have an almost impossible time trying to accomplish my first assignment at my new job. Then you very inconveniently drop in on my new boss, setting the whole office gossiping and my boss wondering what the hell —"

"Amanda," he interrupted softly. He touched his index finger to her lips. "Hush," he whispered.

Amanda jumped up from the couch and turned only when she was three feet away from Eric. "Don't hush me, Eric, and don't touch me!" she cried. "I don't know what you expect, but you're wrong." She narrowed her eyes at him. "No wonder we had that little scene in the bedroom before you told me about all this," she lashed out, her breath coming more quickly now. "It's not terribly easy, in case you don't know, finding out that your ex-husband is involved in dozens of horrible-sounding schemes." Amanda stopped then, stunned suddenly by the shrillness of her voice, the desperate anger that tinged her barrage of ire.

Eric was leaning forward now, stroking his chin. Amanda could see the lines of his temple shift as he clenched and unclenched his jaw. "Maybe we should talk about something else," he said quietly, still not facing her directly.

"Oh, great," Amanda exploded. "That's just great. First you drop a bombshell on me and then you want to change the subject."

"Not entirely," he said softly. "Maybe we should talk about us." And then he looked at her with eyes she suddenly wanted to trust, wanted to believe in, wanted to love.

"Oh, Eric," she said sadly.

He held out a hand. "Come."

She took a deep breath and went and sat next to him on the couch again. She leaned back against the soft cushions and turned to Eric. She felt as if she were suddenly in a haze, a dreamy vagueness she didn't want to leave; it was certainly more comfortable than the shrill anger she had been feeling moments earlier.

"Now listen carefully," he said quietly, almost whispering. "I'm sorry about what's happening with Greg. But it's not my fault, Amanda, and it's not yours either. You're divorced from him, he's a grown man, and if he has any problems, he created them himself. I think what's bothering you most about the whole thing is that you feel guilty. You feel that you might have done something to stop him."

"Well, I might have," she said musingly. "If I had been there for him, if we had still been married . . ."

"Maybe," he answered. "And you'd also have been throwing away your life. Which you were strong enough to realize you didn't want to do, when you finally divorced him. But you have to remember, Amanda — I'm asking you please to try, at least — that whatever happens to Greg — and maybe nothing bad *will* happen — it's not your fault, and it's not mine." His eyes melted into hers. "I want you, Amanda. You know that. I want you as much as any man has ever wanted a woman." The intensity in his eyes was impossible to ignore. "I've dreamed of you countless times." He smiled. "And if I told you what some of those dreams have been, you'd faint dead away." He pursed his lips and held her eyes in his fervid gaze once again. "For now, let's just say we've been good together — incredible together — in my dreams. But we've agreed to go slowly, and we have to separate all of that from Greg and what may or may not happen. It has nothing to do with *us.*"

Amanda sighed and shook her head. "I agree," she said musingly, "but that doesn't mean I'm happy. I have a lot of feelings to sort out." She frowned. "And I guess I don't trust you completely yet, either. A lot has happened in seven years — to both of us — and your ambitions seem to have changed. . . . There's a lot I have to think about."

Eric frowned. "What about my ambitions?" he asked quietly.

"Well" — she shrugged — "I don't think you've been totally open with me about your political ambitions. How come my boss knows more about the nomination than I do?"

Eric sighed and shook his head. "Listen, I think we could go around in circles for the rest of the night, Amanda. It's late, and we're both exhausted."

She sighed. "You're right, I guess," she said reluctantly, and then smiled. "You aren't kicking me out, by any chance, are you?"

He shook his head, suppressing a smile. "Dear God, I never imagined myself doing this in a million years, but yes, Amanda, I am kicking you out."

A few minutes later, as Amanda and Eric stood on the street with a cab waiting, she looked up into his eyes and smiled. "I'm glad we talked, Eric. I'll talk to you tomorrow," she said softly, and wrapped her arms around his neck. Then she closed her eyes and kissed him lightly on the lips as he wrapped his arms around her. She broke the kiss and smiled dreamily. "If I'm really going to leave, I think I'd better get into that cab and actually go before I talk you into changing your mind."

"I think you're right," he said huskily, and kissed her once more, quickly, before letting go of her. "I'll talk to you in the morning," he said, and waited as she got into the cab and drove off.

When Amanda arrived at home, she found a message from Eric asking her to call him. She smiled as she listened to his voice on the tape — low, seductive, with undertones of desire that came through even on the recording.

She sat down on the couch and dialed, still smiling over Eric's having called; it was such a romantic gesture.

But her smile disappeared after the exchange of hellos, when Eric's voice turned serious and distant. "Amanda," he began warily, "I'm sorry to have called. This is very awkward."

"I don't understand," she said quietly, mystified and dreading what might come next. "What's the matter?"

She heard Eric sigh. "Look, I guess all I can say is that I'm sorry. But I'm calling for two reasons."

"Go on," she said, her heart racing.

"Well, to begin with, we didn't discuss your job tonight — your assignment. Needless to say, now that I've told you about Greg, I'm as happy to talk to you as to anyone — obviously. But I wanted to make sure that you understood the confidentiality of the investigation. What I said to you was strictly off the record. If any of it leaks out, we'll both —"

"Do you think I would tell anyone what you told me tonight?" Amanda cut in sharply. "I can't believe my ears, Eric. Did you honestly think it was necessary to tell me our conversation was off the record? Or did you think I might start my report by saying, 'After kissing this reporter rather expertly, Eric Harrison revealed X, Y, and Z'? My God, Eric —"

"There's no need for sarcasm, Amanda. I simply thought that it would be a good idea to remind you —"

"Well, it wasn't!" she snapped.

Eric sighed. "All right," he said. "Never mind, then. I'll talk to you . . . whenever."

Amanda panicked. What did he mean by "whenever"? What had happened to to-morrow morning? "Eric?"

"Yes, Amanda."

"What was the second question you were going to ask me?"

There was a silence. Then he said, "Under the circumstances, Amanda, I think it would be better if we left it alone for now."

Amanda's hopes lifted. The question sounded personal; maybe she and Eric could quickly recapture tonight's mood that had been broken so quickly. "Oh, come on, Eric," she said playfully. "You're talking to Amanda Ellis here, star reporter for WKM. I don't let statements like that alone. If you have a question, shoot."

"All right," he said quietly. "Amanda, did Greg have a silent partner four years ago? Someone who was behind the scenes?"

Amanda swallowed. "What?"

"I asked whether you remembered Greg's —"

"I — I heard you, Eric," she said. "I just can't believe that you'd ask me that kind of a question."

He was silent.

"Don't you see why?" she cried. "You're asking me to contribute to the prosecution of my own ex-husband. My God, I might not still be in love with him, but I certainly don't want to send him to prison." She closed her eyes and took a deep breath before she spoke her next words. "Eric, I can't think straight. I hope it's because I'm exhausted. But all I know is that right now I don't want to talk to you, and I don't know when I will. I'm sorry."

And she hung up before he could say anything else.

Chapter Six

What hurt Amanda most as she began to calm down after hanging up was the nagging thought that Eric had wanted to ask her that awful question all night long. It was difficult to imagine, but the thought kept returning, unbidden, like a recurring nightmare. She readied herself for bed with an automaticity born of the deep confusion she felt, her mind racing through speculation after speculation, question after question. As soon as she got into bed, she realized she was wide awake — an infuriating condition given the fact that she had had three hours' sleep the night before — and the tears that began to run down her cheeks were tears of exhaustion as well as of frustration and sadness.

Parts of the evening had been wonderful — moments she had dreamed of, like when she and Eric had kissed, when he had told her how he dreamed of her, when he had kissed her again outside his building. Most cherished of all the moments was when Eric had spoken freely of his feelings; he had seemed so honest then, more like the Eric she remembered than at any other time.

And as the tears flowed, Amanda silently protested that those moments had to have been real; they had not been merely preludes to that awful question, diversions or distractions that would make Amanda more ready and willing to supply Eric with information about Greg. No, those moments had been real, and Eric's words had been genuine, from the heart. Also, she could not let herself forget that those eyes of his never lied, and she had seen sincerity and honesty and perhaps even love in those eyes tonight.

Yet, if Eric had meant all he had said earlier, didn't his asking about Greg afterward mean that he lacked a certain sensitivity? Amanda tried to imagine a situation in which the tables were turned, but she couldn't; her feelings about Greg were the key, and Eric had no analogous feelings for anyone in his life that she knew of.

Perhaps what she had recently feared about Eric was true: perhaps he felt success was essential at all costs, and his driving ambition had blinded him to all emotions, feelings, and considerations. Or perhaps she had wanted so much to believe that something wonderful could happen between her and Eric that she had deluded herself about his sincerity, his honesty, his integrity. Perhaps she had simply tried to make a fantasy come true and had ignored the realities until now. Finding Eric free after all these years had held the promise of realizing her fantasies, and perhaps of true happiness as well. She had to admit, now, as she contemplated the problem with care, that in her excitement over future possibilities, she might have imagined what wasn't in fact true. Perhaps Eric simply wasn't the man she had thought he was. Yes, he had been sincere at times tonight, but he also had revealed to her shadings of his personality that she had never glimpsed before. She had cherished, after all, a mental image of Eric over the past seven years, and that image had probably become idealized as time had passed. Now she had to force herself to shed that beautiful image in favor of reality, no matter how bleak it was in comparison.

Amanda finally fell into a deep and troubled sleep, awakening many times during the night to have her pleasant dreams of Eric blackened by reality. It struck her as odd that her dreams were beautiful — romantic and idyllic encounters with Eric, the kind he had referred to that evening. Why wasn't she having nightmares, nightmares of Eric tricking her, Eric lying, Eric twisting the truth? Were her dreams trying to tell her something? she wondered sleepily.

In the morning she looked back on the night's dreams with cynicism. And by the time she arrived at work, she knew what she had to do. She'd have to beg off the commission story — not because of her half involvement with Eric, but because of Greg's possible guilt. For, though she was using her maiden name again, it simply wouldn't do to have her on a story covering her own ex-husband. Stan would whisk her off the story himself if he knew, and since he had no way of knowing and Amanda was not going to break Eric's confidence, she'd have to take herself off the story without Stan's help or understanding. He was sure to think she was demurring because of a romantic involvement, but that was a falsity she would simply have to accept and live with.

She marched into Stan's office before going to her own.

"Stan," she began, "I'd like you to assign coverage of the Harrison Commission and the close-up on Eric to someone else."

Stan frowned. "Why?" He motioned brusquely for her to sit down.

"I'm afraid it's personal," Amanda stated flatly, her tone indicating that she'd say no more and answer no questions.

Stan sighed. "A reporter can be involved

with a subject, Amanda, at this level of coverage. It's not unheard of. And it's not as if you're writing editorials about Harrison."

Amanda shook her head. "That isn't the problem, Stan. But it is a personal one, and I'd appreciate it if you could see your way clear to assigning someone else." She swallowed. "I know I'm taking a chance asking you to do something like this on my first assignment, but I've decided it's better to take *this* chance with myself than to force the station to take a chance on my story."

Stan studied her for a few moments and then frowned. "Look, Amanda, I'll say yes if you insist. But I don't want to — you did a great job on the first press conference."

Amanda smiled. "Thanks. But I do insist. And I promise you this won't happen again."

Stan nodded and shrugged and, after telling Amanda to go see Carlotta Somers for another assignment at ten o'clock, dismissed her.

When Amanda arrived at her office, there was a message from Eric asking her to call, and Amanda tried to ignore the leap of happiness her heart took. She would have to call Eric and explain that she had asked to be taken off the story without giving any explanation. She herself didn't know whether she couldn't face doing the story because of confusion over Eric or its focus on Greg, but she did know her decision had been an intelligent one, and she would abide by it no matter what Eric said.

She was put through to Eric immediately. "Amanda," he said.

"Yes, good morning," she said, her voice softening despite her resolves.

"Amanda, I'm sorry about last night. It was tactless, and I should have stuck with my decision not to use you in any way in our investigation of Greg."

"Well, it wasn't the most pleasant situation in the world," she said quietly.

"Especially after our conversation," Eric finished. "Listen, Amanda, I'm incredibly busy today, but I thought it might be a good day for you to come down and do some talking with Sheila. Since I *did* interrupt you two so precipitously yesterday, and you do have a story to get out."

"I'm off the story, Eric," she said quickly, before she could change her mind. "I asked to be taken off both stories this morning, and Stan agreed."

"Dammit, Amanda," Eric barked, "what in hell did you do that for?"

"Don't get angry," she said. "You sound as if I wanted to do it. I didn't. But it was the

148

wisest thing I could have done at the time, and I'm abiding by my decision."

"What reason did you give?" he asked quietly.

"No reason," she snapped. "Just personal with no explanations."

"Wonderful," Eric said sarcastically. "That's a very professional tack to take with your first assignment."

"I gave it a lot of thought," she said quaveringly, though she had meant to make a strong statement.

"So did I!" Eric exploded. "Why in hell do you think I broke all the rules of the investigation, if not to tell you about Greg so that we wouldn't have a lie hanging between us every time you interviewed me? Amanda, I would have vastly preferred not to tell you about Greg, but I did it because I hoped we could go *on* with the story then — not end it. You can cover the commission with no problems now that I don't have to hide anything from you. We don't know if Greg is guilty, and at this point it's much more important for you to do well at your job."

Amanda sighed and closed her eyes, wishing she could close her ears to Eric's words so that she could think it all through by herself. Somehow she hadn't ever considered Eric's motives for having told her about Greg. She had attacked Eric for not having told her sooner, yet she had never looked into the reasons why he finally did.

"Amanda?"

"Yes, Eric."

"When you hang up, just march right back into Stan's office and say you've changed your mind. And do it fast, before he gives the assignment to someone else. Stan thinks I'm a hot subject, even if no one else does."

Amanda smiled for a moment and then shook her head. "I can't, Eric. That really *would* look unprofessional. You know that."

Eric sighed. "You certainly have gotten us into a mess, Mandy. All right. Just leave it to me. Call me back in half an hour, and I'll have the whole thing set up."

He hung up before she could ask what he planned, but she was thinking not of that but of two things he had just said, two things that made her heart sing: He had called her "Mandy," which he hadn't done in seven years, and he had said "us," that she had gotten *them* — together — into a mess.

Amanda smiled and sank back into her chair. *This* Eric, the Eric who called her Mandy and considered them an "us," this was the Eric she cared for and wanted to be with.

A few minutes later Amanda saw Stan making his way through the clutter of newsroom desks, heading straight for Amanda's office. She couldn't read his expression, but he didn't look overjoyed. She sat up in her chair and began typing up the notes she had made on Eric so far. If someone else was going to take over the story, she would give him or her whatever she had so far.

Stan let himself in to her office and eased himself into the chair across from her. "All right," he said, looking at Amanda steadily. "I'm going to make a switch one more time, Amanda."

She tried not to smile. "I — did you speak with Eric?"

"Yes, I spoke with Harrison," he said impatiently, "and that stubborn son of a bitch won't speak with anyone from WKM but you, which means no close-up unless you go back on the story."

"I see," Amanda said slowly. "I guess I'm back on the story then."

Stan shrugged. "Unless whatever 'personal' considerations you have are too strong." He looked at her skeptically. "I gather you're not against going back on the story." He raised an eyebrow. "The way your face lit up when you heard what Harrison said, it isn't too difficult to see what you want."

Amanda's cheeks flamed. "I *am* sorry, Stan — about all of this. It won't happen again."

Stan stood up and pointed a finger at Amanda. "You're right about *that*, Amanda, because I won't let it happen again. You get your personal problems straightened out. Good as you are, you're not irreplaceable." His face softened. "I don't want to belabor the point, but I want you to understand very clearly. This is the last time. So you tell me. Are you on the story or off? If you're off, we'll go ahead without Harrison's cooperation. It's not the way I like to do things, but it's certainly been done before."

Amanda took a deep breath. "I'm on the story," she said, to herself as much as to Stan. "I'm on, Stan, and I promise you'll get two good stories. I promise."

Half an hour later Amanda was on her way to Eric's office in a taxi, hoping against hope that she had made the correct decision. When she walked into Eric's office a few minutes later, she suspected she had chosen right.

Eric was leaning back in his chair with his shoes up on the edge of the desk, looking at Amanda with a mixture of pleasure and faint mockery. "Well," he said, eyes flashing and lips curled in mild amusement. "I'm certainly glad we got all *that* straightened out, Amanda."

He swung his long legs down off the desk and unbuttoned the cuffs of his pale pink shirt, rolling up the sleeves to expose thickly muscled forearms dark with hair. "Now we have some work to do. Sit," he commanded, gesturing toward the chair next to his.

As Eric riffled through some papers, Amanda sat down, piling her materials on the desk. Eric gave her an ironic look of annoyance as she did so, but turned back to his work.

Amanda watched in silence as Eric scanned the contents of a folder in front of him, his dark brows coming together in irritation as he shook his head. "God damn it," he swore softly, and angrily turned to another page of whatever he was reading.

Normally, Amanda would have been annoyed over a situation in which she was sitting silently, watching someone whom she was supposed to be interviewing just reading to himself. But she was mesmerized by the intensity of Eric's concentration — his lips pursed, his dark eyes shadowed by long lashes, his massive chest impatiently expanding and contracting like that of a bull aching to get out of the starting box and into the ring. He swore under his breath and turned to Amanda, shaking his head. "You reporters," he rasped. "You really know how to throw expert little wrenches into the works."

Amanda sat up straighter, girding herself to respond to what sounded like another on-slaught of anger. "Just what are you refer-ring to?" she said cautiously.

Eric impatiently shook his head, a lock of black hair falling down over his forehead. "I'm not talking about you," he snarled, im-patiently pushing his hair back. "I'm talking about the *Herald*. They must pick up their information from sewer rats."

"What are you talking about, exactly?" Amanda asked, surprised and a bit cowed by the intensity of Eric's wrath.

"Some damn reporter," he muttered, "has me in as a definite candidate for the Democratic nomination — a 'shoo-in,' he says."

Amanda looked at him blankly. "Is that all? That doesn't sound so terrible to me," she said calmly. "If it's true — which appar-ently it's not — you shouldn't mind. And if it's not true, having that sort of complimen-tary item printed about you isn't so awful. It can't look bad to the partners at your firm or to the —"

"Dammit, Amanda," he swore. "Don't you reporters think of the impact of anything before you print it or broadcast it or announce it? A nomination is a very delicate process — very delicate. And premature announcements of success or assumed success can knock dozens of people's noses out of joint — dozens of people you need for the nomination, who get more than a little teed off that the candidate didn't see fit to consult them or keep them up to date or solicit their thoughts." He hit the desk with the folder and then threw himself angrily back into his chair, turning his back to Amanda.

"Eric," Amanda said quietly.

He whirled around and took her in with an angry gaze that seemed also surprised; it was as if Eric had been talking more to himself than to Amanda. "What is it?" he said, the gruffness almost gone from his voice.

"Does all of this mean that you *are,* in fact, seeking the nomination?" She looked at him curiously. "Somehow I don't think you'd be this upset over the 'delicacy' of the matter if you didn't want the nomination very much."

Eric's dark eyes sparked angrily. "No, it does not 'mean' that. Necessarily." He sighed, and his hardened features relaxed. "I just don't know, Amanda," he said, shaking his head. "But having the news media interfere isn't making my decision any easier."

"Then you *are* considering going after the nomination," Amanda persisted.

"Obviously," he snapped, and then looked at her with regret. "I'm sorry. Yes, I *am* still considering it. But, Amanda, I'm telling that to you as a friend, not as a reporter. If you want to use it for the record, go ahead, but you be damn careful that you get it right."

Amanda swallowed and nodded. "Don't worry," she said flatly, sounding calmer than she felt. Although Eric had said he was only "considering" the nomination, it was now eminently clear that he wanted it very much and this disturbed Amanda deeply, in ways she didn't even want to consider at the moment. "When do you plan to make a final decision?" she asked quietly.

"The decision isn't up to me. That's why I'm upset. I may lose the nomination if enough articles and reports like this *Herald* article come out."

"But you do have to make a decision if they decide to nominate you," she said gently, and paused. "You could always say no."

His eyes looked into hers then, trying to

read them, to divine what the Amanda behind those blue eyes was thinking. Eric looked down, his dark lashes fringed against rough cheeks, his lips pursed in thought. And when he looked up again, his eyes were rueful, dark and clear and filled with regret and reluctance. "I could always say no," he said musingly. "It's true, I could always say no."

And they continued to look into each other's eyes, speaking volumes though no words were spoken, as he said it was something he had to do, and she said how much she didn't want him to do it, and both said they wanted to be together without this problem or past problems or future problems that seemed constantly to keep them apart.

"Look," he said gently. "I really haven't made up my mind yet."

Amanda nodded, her eyes still gazing into his, and said, "Good," though she knew he had simply said it to please her, and because he wished it were true.

Eric took a deep breath and set his hands on the desk. "Well," he said briskly, "enough soul-searching. I'm due downtown at eleven, and it must be —"

The intercom on the desk buzzed, and as Amanda looked at her watch and discovered it was already after eleven o'clock, Eric was apparently discovering the same piece of news from Sheila Farnham.

"Dammit, Sheila," he snapped. "Obviously I *am* here, and obviously I *haven't* left! I wish you would check earlier in the future." And he slammed the phone down, shaking his head. "Sheila is a brilliant press aide, but when it comes to secretarial duties I'd do better with no one. I should learn not to rely on her for that sort of thing."

"Why don't you just hire a secretary?" Amanda asked, as Eric hastily gathered up some papers on his desk and crammed them into an already full briefcase.

"The commission has a limited budget," he said matter-of-factly. And then he grinned. "And anyway, if you work things right, you can get people to do what you want without their even realizing it."

Amanda stared. "I don't think I like the sound of that statement or its implications."

He raised an eyebrow and shrugged. "Oh, come now, Amanda. As a reporter you've done that a thousand times over." He frowned. "I'm not talking about having people do things they really don't want to do. I'm talking about getting people to do things they really don't mind, or things they want to do but are afraid to try." He shrugged. "Nothing harmful. Just slightly —"

"Try deceitful," Amanda cut in. She slung her purse over her shoulder and gathered up her briefcase and still-unused tape recorder from the desk. "And I guess I might as well come along and see you in action as you convince a cast of thousands to do things they don't want to do."

Eric smiled. "I certainly hope you're joking, Amanda. If I turn on the news and see you saying anything of the kind" — he raised an eyebrow — "there'll be hell to pay."

Amanda flashed her eyes in challenge. "As long as you watch WKM, Eric, that's all I care about." She shrugged. "And as long as you're talking people into doing things they don't want to do, why don't you talk a few people into watching WKM?"

He winked. "Maybe I will. Especially with you covering the commission. Great press never hurt, you know."

Amanda frowned as Eric held the door for her and she preceded him out of his office. She wished he hadn't mentioned her coverage of the commission again. Did he judge everyone by how much they could do for him and treat them accordingly? It didn't seem likely — not with the Eric she knew —

but anything was possible now.

Eric pulled a brown tweed jacket off the hat rack next to Sheila's desk and hurriedly put it on.

"I'm sorry I didn't tell you it was time to leave, Eric," Sheila said, looking up at him adoringly as he ran a tie through his collar. "Here, let me help," she cried, and within seconds had jumped up from her desk and was working Eric's tie through his collar.

Amanda watched with growing annoyance as Sheila stood close in front of Eric, carefully and slowly tying his tie, laughing and saying she had to do it again, untying it before Eric could stop her, her young cheeks flaming as she laughed and looked up at him, her dark brown eyes saying more, Amanda realized, than Amanda had ever let her eyes say to Eric. Sheila's adoration of Eric was just that — simple, uncomplicated love, or infatuation, perhaps, but in any case pure and unwavering. And Eric didn't seem to mind, Amanda observed. His usually hard features were set in a look of not-quite appreciation but certainly more than tolerance; his dark eyes were velvety and warm; his lips just barely suppressed a smile.

When Sheila was finally finished, Eric cleared his throat and shook a finger at her. "Now listen carefully, Sheila. I know you're drafting the news release this afternoon, but this is more important at the moment. Call Hal Jenkins and tell him I'm on my way, with a reporter. And do it now. I'll see you tomorrow. I'll be meeting with the DA this afternoon after I see Jenkins, and I probably won't be back. I'll call in later, though, so be here."

"Right," Sheila said, and then she suddenly clapped her hand over her mouth and her eyes widened in fear. "Oh, no," she murmured, looking at Eric as if she were terrified of him. "I forgot."

"Forgot what?" Eric barked.

Sheila looked at her watch. "Never mind. I'll have time to take care of it," she said quietly, sounding less sure than she no doubt wanted to.

"Forgot what?" Eric persisted.

Sheila sighed. "The DA called a little while ago and said he wanted you to bring those papers — the drafts — with you this afternoon."

Eric's eyes flashed daggers at her. "Why the hell didn't you tell me that before, Sheila?"

"I forgot," she cried. "I'm sorry." She paused. "Are they still at your apartment?"

"*Yes,* they're still at my apartment," Eric fumed, looking at his watch.

"I could go for you," Sheila said hopefully. "On my lunch hour, if you give me the key."

Eric appeared to consider her suggestion for a few moments, and then glanced at Amanda. "No. That's all right, Sheila. I'll work it out. I should have made sure to bring the papers in today myself." He gave her an affectionate pat on the shoulder. "You stick around here and hold down the fort, and I'll call you later."

The early autumn wind blew Eric's and Amanda's hair as the two hurried along Fifth Avenue to the Rockefeller Center office of Hal Jenkins, a public-relations man who had just successfully managed the mayor's re-election campaign. Eric had stopped the taxi ten blocks short of the destination when he had seen that he and Amanda could get where they wanted to go more quickly by walking, and now Amanda was racing along, trying to keep pace with Eric's long strides.

It was the first time in seven years that Amanda had been in this part of the city with Eric, only two blocks from their old office, and the familiar sights and smells and sounds — of horns blaring, blue sky just visible past the towering skyscrapers, milling groups of tourists walking at a snail's pace

162

compared to the native New Yorkers — brought back a rush of fond memories to Amanda.

As they hurried along, Eric turned to Amanda and smiled. "I love the smell of New York at this time of year" — he laughed — "and *only* this time of year — with the hot chestnuts and pretzels for sale on every corner."

"Mm," Amanda agreed, smiling at a memory. "Remember when we walked thirty blocks that night to find one of those vendors?" She frowned. "I can't remember what we were even looking for."

Eric smiled. "*I* do, and you should because it was *your* craving, Mandy. At eleven at night, and you said you were going on strike unless I went out and found you a hot pretzel. Nothing else would do, you said."

She laughed. "Now I remember. And we didn't go back, did we? I mean to the office."

They stopped at the curb, and Eric turned and looked at her with dark eyes filled with longing. "No, we didn't go back," he said musingly. "I finally convinced you that an early breakfast at the Brasserie would be a passable second choice to a hot pretzel."

The light changed, and the crowd pushed Eric and Amanda onward, forcing each to remember that night privately. It had been one of the loveliest nights of Amanda's life, and one of the most disappointing as well; for after she and Eric had shared a breakfast of bacon and eggs and crusty French bread and steaming, rich coffee, Amanda had returned to her home, and Eric to his, each once again alone.

She looked up at Eric now — striding along, tall against the crowd, the wind blowing his dark hair gently back from his forehead — and she felt a wave of terrible guilt, as if it were seven years ago and she and Eric were both still married.

And seconds later, when Eric guided her into the lobby of the RCA Building, he stopped and looked down at her with an unreadable expression and said almost sadly, "It all brings back a lot of memories, doesn't it?"

Not believing that Eric's thought processes could possibly have been traveling on such a similar track as her own, Amanda said, "What do you mean?"

His gaze was unwavering. "I think you know exactly what I mean," he said. "I feel as if it's seven years ago, and we both still work at Parker, Holeywell." He reached forward and held Amanda's shoulders. "Or more to the point, Amanda, that we're both still married, wanting each other and thinking of nothing else almost every waking minute."

Her lips parted as he continued to speak.

"Amanda, something has shifted in me . . . changed somehow." He paused. "Just look at us, at what we're doing. We're together, right now . . . nearly in the same place as we were seven years ago." He shook his head, his gaze never leaving hers. "But we're apart," he said softly. "And I don't want that."

Amanda had to look away from Eric then, for it was impossible to concentrate — even to speak — with those deep brown eyes penetrating hers, promising her something she had wanted for seven long years. She looked down at the floor. "Eric, I —"

He reached out and gently tilted her chin up toward his face. "I want to see your eyes when you speak, Mandy."

She shook her head and closed her eyes. "No."

"Yes," he said gently, and when she opened her eyes and looked into his, she knew the words she was about to speak would be among the most difficult of her life. "Eric, this is very hard for me," she began. "What you just said — that you want to be with me — is something I love to hear — I loved hearing you tell me that the other

165

night." She smiled wistfully. "Our being here . . . together . . . brought back memories for me, too, but they were memories that were . . . different." She paused. "Suddenly I'm feeling guilty for the feelings we had for each other back then. Perhaps guiltier now than I felt then. Think about what we're doing, how we met recently, and why. I just don't think I could live with seeing you — as a lover — while you have the investigation still going on. Somehow it would make me part of something I don't want to be a part of."

"Mandy, your feelings of guilt — those are coming back from the past, not the present."

"But *think* of the present, Eric," she said quietly. "There's just something . . . wrong, I guess, about my getting together with you now." She shook her head. "It would make me feel horribly guilty."

Eric's jaw clenched. "Mandy, don't you see what you're doing? We're repeating our relationship of seven years ago, preventing our love because of fear, not because it's wrong, not because we don't want it. That's what I was thinking about as we were walking along the street and I began to remember all those times, all those nights. And days. And dreams."

Amanda pulled out of his grasp and began to walk away, but Eric caught her and turned her around. "I'm serious, Mandy."

Someone bumped into Eric then, and suddenly Amanda was aware of where they were, why they were there, and how late they were for Eric's appointment. "Eric, we must be really late," she said.

Eric glared at her. "I don't give a damn how late we are, or if we never get there. This is more important."

"I'm sorry, Eric, but I know the meeting is very important to you — maybe more important than you realize — and I think we should go." She broke away from his grip. "I'm going, anyway, so you might as well come along."

Eric scowled at her and she turned away, making her way through the crowded lobby for the elevator. When Eric caught up with her, he was smiling skeptically. "You'd better watch it," he muttered as they waited in a small knot of people for the elevator.

"Oh?" she said coyly, trying to lighten the mood. "Why is that?"

Then, when her eyes met his, she saw he was serious. "Because you *do* know what's important to me, Mandy, and that's just one more reason I'm not going to let you get away from me this time."

They exchanged a look that made Amanda's knees go weak, and then once again were pulled out of their haze by an impatient crowd pushing its way into the elevator.

Chapter Seven

In Hal Jenkins's office Amanda hardly heard a word that passed between him and Eric after the initial introductions were made. Though she was sitting not far from either one, she heard little and saw only Eric — his challenging eyes, ready smile, and easy gestures. It would be so easy, Amanda knew, to submit to the physical longings she had resisted for so long, to fall into Eric's arms and feel his warm, hard body in all its strength. Yet she knew, too, that with the passion and ecstasy would also come remorse and guilt and regret.

She had been honest with him when she had explained her feelings, as he had been honest with her; yet now, as she looked at him laughing and talking, expertly directing the meeting, she desperately wished that what she had said to Eric were a lie. Yet it was a truth from which she could not hide. And now, even if she wanted to hide from her own feelings, and lie to herself in order to be with this man she had wanted for years, now that she had told Eric of her feelings, she suspected — indeed, knew — that he would not let her lie to herself, ever.

Sudden loud laughter cut through Amanda's thoughts, and she realized that Eric and Jenkins were both looking at her.

Eric had on his maddeningly confident smile, and his eyes were sparked with spirit. "Well, what do you think?" he queried, lazily crossing his long legs and leaning back in his chair. "Would this make the men and women of New York flock to the polls to vote for me?" He held up an eight-by-ten mock-up of a campaign poster, a photo of himself with his name emblazoned in red diagonally across the lower half, along with the words A VOTE FOR INTEGRITY. It was one of the photographs Sheila had taken, that Amanda had seen back at the commission headquarters. It was an attractive picture, to be sure, with Eric looking like a respectable but approachable politician. But Amanda hated it; it was the perfect representation of what she didn't want Eric to become.

"More to the point," Jenkins suddenly said, "will that picture send the *women* flocking to the polls to vote for Eric?"

Amanda looked at Jenkins to see if he was joking, but his self-satisfied grin told her that he was serious, though incidentally pleased with himself as well. Amanda turned to Eric, who looked merely amused, his lips curled in mild pleasure.

"Seriously, Miss Ellis," Jenkins prodded, "you're an attractive young woman, a member of the voting public of this city, I presume. You'd vote for this guy after seeing this picture enough times, wouldn't you?"

Amanda glared at Jenkins. "If you plan to run a campaign on the basis of looks, Mr. Jenkins, why not just plaster centerfolds of Eric all over the city?" she sputtered angrily. "Why not go all the way?" she cried.

As soon as the words were out, Amanda wished she had said anything — *any*thing — other than what she had said. Jenkins was staring at her — first as if she were crazy, and then as if, suddenly struck with inspiration, he were actually considering the idea. But Eric was the one she wished hadn't heard her words, for he was laughing, leaning back in his chair and laughing deeply, and he laughed so long and so hard that his dark lashes became wet with tears.

Amanda, wishing he would stop, cleared her throat and was about to speak when Eric suddenly stood up. Still laughing a bit, he wiped his eyes and shook his head, then stepped forward and extended his hand to Jenkins. "You know, Jenkins," he said, "I

171

know you're one of the best PR men in the city — and I don't want you to take this as a personal affront" — he raised a brow — "but Miss Ellis here has hit the nail right on the head."

Jenkins looked from Eric to Amanda and back to Eric again, his brows knit in confusion. "What do you mean?"

Eric smiled. "I mean that your approach to my campaign — if I have a campaign — is based just a little too much on looks and 'charisma,' as you keep calling it, for my taste."

Jenkins glared at him. "Say no more, Harrison," he said gruffly. "I've heard it all before. And you know who from? From losers, people whose names you've forgotten along with everyone else in this city."

Eric raised a brow. "That may be," he said evenly. "But I'll take my chances on a campaign run the way I want to run it."

Jenkins scoffed and rolled his eyes. "Were you born yesterday, Harrison? Is that it? You really expect the voters to pay attention to the issues? Sex is what sells, Harrison. Sex and charisma."

"I'll take my chances on the issues," Eric said steadily. "I wouldn't want to win an election any other way."

Jenkins slowly shook his head. "I'm sorry

to hear that, Harrison. Real sorry."

Eric shrugged philosophically. "It's good to find out our differences as early on as possible, Jenkins. And it *has* been good working with you. Please send your bill to my downtown office."

"Right," Jenkins said dejectedly. "I'll do that."

Once out of the office, Eric put his arm around Amanda and held her close, looking down into her eyes and smiling. "You're a godsend on top of everything else," he said, shaking his head. "I'd met with that guy three or four times, and I hadn't realized what he was doing until you made that little unforgettable barb."

Amanda's cheeks flamed. "Do me a favor and try to forget it, Eric."

He raised an eyebrow. "But whatever for? I'd like to contemplate the whole thing for a little while." His eyes glowed. "You could take some preliminary shots, Amanda. Who knows? Maybe it *is* a good idea at that."

Amanda laughed nervously, acutely conscious of the fact that she was still blushing and probably wouldn't stop until the subject was changed.

"Well?" Eric prodded.

"I *don't* think so." Amanda smiled, but her

smile faded when her eyes met his and she saw how serious he had become. His eyes shone with a heat that made her ache for him.

"Amanda," he said softly, "it's easy to joke with you, but I think we should talk. Seriously, I mean. About us." His unfathomable dark eyes glowed with a thousand promises. "I want to be with you," he murmured. "And make love for hours and hours and hours, for as long as it takes to make up for the years of wanting, the years of waiting," he said huskily. "I don't want to wait any longer."

Amanda turned away. From down the hall a young woman was coming toward them, giving Eric a long look of appraisal. She passed and went into one of the offices as Eric spoke again. "Amanda," he said softly.

"I — I don't know," Amanda said, afraid to turn around and face him. It was so difficult to say no when she looked into those eyes, gazed at those lips, melted into his hungry gaze. "I can't talk about it now."

He came forward then and gently touched her shoulder. "All right," he said softly. "For now."

Amanda wondered how long she would be able to resist Eric's yearning words and longing touches. When she thought of the heated union they had almost fulfilled at Eric's house — his urgent graspings, coaxing tongue, exploring hands, throbbing desire — she wondered why she even wanted to resist, even considered resisting. But part of her knew, too, that the love-making could not exist in a vacuum, nor would she want it to. She simply wasn't ready to give herself up to Eric in all the ways that would accompany physical love. She was painfully aware that she was avoiding discussing — or even privately thinking about — Eric's political plans and how they could affect the relationship. For as a political reporter she couldn't possibly involve herself with a candidate for the Senate. And what of her feelings of guilt about being involved with Eric during his investigation of Greg? Why couldn't she rid herself of the years-old guilt that had inextricably merged with new, even more powerful feelings of culpability? She wanted this man — had wanted him for years. Why couldn't she forget her feelings and simply follow her heart's yearnings?

Yet she knew — as he knew — that would never happen. She had never done that sort of thing in the past, and she wasn't about to start now; she simply didn't believe in giving herself fully to a man without full love —

with no guilt — on both sides.

Amanda set her troubled musings aside when she and Eric parted in the lobby to call their respective offices. There were no late-breaking assignments Amanda had to cover, so she was free to spend the rest of the day working on the close-up on Eric.

When Eric finished talking on the phone — apparently with Sheila, Amanda guessed, judging by the smile on Eric's face that was probably totally unconscious — he had an odd look in his eyes, as if he were undecided about something.

"Uh, listen," he said, glancing at his watch. "Sheila had the DA push the appointment back to four o'clock, so I'm going to have time to go up to my place for the papers before going." He paused. "Why don't you come along?"

"Oh, I don't think —"

"You haven't eaten lunch," Eric persisted. "And you do have a story to do."

"For which I could probably get more information from your staff than from you."

He gave her a sidelong glance of disbelief. "You wouldn't want to get your information from a bunch of star-struck kids, would you, when you can get it from the horse's mouth?"

Amanda smiled. "Star-struck! Don't tell

me you're beginning to believe your fans and followers, that you're a star."

"And don't tell *me* you're not trying to change the subject, Amanda. Now as far as I'm concerned, it's settled. You can't come along to the meeting with the DA — that's confidential to the nth degree no matter how I feel about it — so coming along with me before then is going to be your best shot at uninterrupted time with me."

Amanda grinned. "I see. And this 'uninterrupted time' is to be used for research purposes?"

"Of course," Eric joked. "I have only your best professional interests at heart, my dear."

Despite her professional resolves, Amanda accomplished little in the way of interviewing during the taxi ride. Eric seemed preoccupied, and after a few questions Amanda dropped the subject of politics in favor of small talk. But Eric seemed more distracted still.

Once in Eric's apartment Amanda felt more comfortable about the idea of finally interviewing him seriously; at last they had some privacy and, as he had mentioned, some uninterrupted time. But Eric cut her off as soon as she opened her mouth. "First," he said briskly, "a little help in the kitchen. Then we can talk."

Amanda's planned protests were silenced when Eric began taking food out of the refrigerator and she realized how hungry she was.

"Omelets okay?" Eric asked.

"Absolutely," Amanda agreed enthusiastically. "Here, let me help."

And together they prepared the lunch, Amanda chopping up bits of scallions and pepperoni and Eric beating the eggs and preparing the French bread, which he sliced halfway through in thick slices, spread with butter, and put in the oven.

"White wine would be nice, but I need every ounce of my mental strength for my meeting with the DA," Eric said.

Amanda nodded; she needed every ounce of mental strength for her meeting right now. "Coffee would be great," she said.

A few minutes later Amanda and Eric were sitting on the couch in the living room eating delicious omelets with hot crusty bread and steaming coffee. "Mm," Amanda said, "this is great."

"I'm glad you like it," Eric said, smiling. "It's meant to impress. Omelets are one of my specialties."

"Well, I *am* impressed," Amanda answered, swallowing another delicious mouthful.

Eric leaned back and spread his arms across the tops of the cushions. "Now," he said. "I think I have a promise to fulfill."

"What's that?" Amanda asked.

"I promised you some time, and I'm ready to talk now, if you'd like." He gazed at her with soft brown eyes. "I honestly haven't tried to make things difficult for you, Mandy, but I know I have."

Amanda nodded slowly. "All right, let's talk. But I'm going to turn on the tape recorder, okay? I don't absolutely have to, but it makes things a lot easier."

Eric frowned. "All right. I suppose I can see your point."

Amanda smiled. "Good." She set up the recorder on the coffee table, flicked it on, and turned to Eric. "Now. How serious are your political plans at this point, Eric? It's a question everyone seems to be interested in, and I think the public has a right to know — *your* plans and *your* feelings, Eric, not what other people's intentions are. I understand you'd rather not comment on them at the moment."

Eric slowly shook his head, his dark eyes smiling. "You certainly can turn it on and off, Mandy. You sound as impersonal as any reporter I've ever met," he marveled.

"It's my job, Eric."

"All right," he sighed, running his fingers back through his glossy hair. "The best answer I can give at this point is to say that I'm not certain either way at the moment. Naturally, one crucial element is the length of the commission's investigation. If it's going to take me past the point at which I'd want to begin campaigning, then obviously I'd say no." He paused. "There would be other reasons I'd say no, too."

"Such as?"

"Personal reasons."

Their eyes met, and Amanda looked away quickly, unnerved by the intensity of Eric's velvety eyes.

"Eric, how do you explain your statement at the press conference a few days ago, which clearly indicated you had no interest in politics?"

A glimmer of a smile played on Eric's lips. "At the time I hadn't heard that several leading Democrats had gotten together to push for my nomination. It never seemed as possible as it does now."

Amanda nodded, silent. Eric had a light in his eyes, an excitement she used to see when he was fired up about trying a case he felt passionately about. "Eric," she said quietly, reaching forward and turning off the tape recorder, "you really want the nomination, don't you?"

He shrugged philosophically. "I honestly don't know, Amanda. It's all happened so quickly." He glanced down at the tape recorder. "Why did you turn that off?"

Amanda looked down, studying her hands. "I . . . don't want what I'm going to say to be on the tape, Eric."

She looked up at him and his eyes darkened. "Go on," he said cautiously.

She cleared her throat. "Well, this isn't easy for me to say, Eric. . . ."

"Say anything you like," he said gently.

She smiled. "All right. I . . . you spoke of our being together."

"Yes," he said quietly, his eyes locked with hers.

"I . . . know I said no, at least for now."

"Go on," he murmured.

"I still know that I'm not quite ready, Eric. . . . But that doesn't mean that it's no forever. Or even for a very long time."

Eric frowned. "But — ?"

"But there's a problem . . . another problem. If we did begin to see each other . . . seriously, it would create complications for me professionally."

"I don't understand."

"If you ran for office, Eric. Or for the nomination, even. Don't you see? I'm a *po-*

litical reporter." She shook her head. "I'd be out of that area immediately if we were involved with each other and you were more than what you are now — politically, I mean."

Eric paled, and he leaned his head back and looked up at the ceiling.

"Eric?"

He glanced over at her and then simply looked upward again, quietly uttering a whispered oath. Then, when he sat up and looked at her, his eyes were full of pain. "I suppose," he said slowly, "I suppose the problem just slipped right past me because I haven't thought about you much in terms of your career, Amanda." He smiled sadly. "To me you're just Amanda, the woman I've been thinking about for a long time." He shook his head. "I've never thought of you as 'Amanda Ellis, WKM-TV.' " He held up a palm. "And please don't take that as any sort of insult, Mandy. I no more think of you as a reporter than you think of me as a senator."

Amanda knit her brows. "I understand," she said sadly, "although I wish I didn't. . . . I wish this weren't happening." She sighed and looked away from Eric, out the windows and across the river. The sky was gray, as was the river, and Amanda felt as if they would be gray forever, as gray as her heart would be heavy.

"Amanda," Eric murmured, gently caressing her cheek with the back of his hand. "Nothing is definite. My political career is as up in the air as can be, and . . . well, you're not going to do political reporting forever."

Amanda whipped around to face him. "This is my *career*, not just a job," she flared, "and though you may not have decided where you're going, Eric, I have. I don't intend to make any changes."

He gazed at her hair, her eyes, her lips. "Mandy," he said softly. "Don't. Don't worry, and don't be upset. As I look at you now — at your eyes, those eyes I've dreamed of, and those lips — I can't imagine anything I'd want to do more than be with you. I know we can work it out."

Amanda closed her eyes. "That's — that's what you say now, Eric. But you don't know how you'll feel when you're surrounded by admirers and well-wishers, people whose only goal is to make you successful. And I don't want to be responsible for killing that dream of yours, Eric."

Gently he brushed his hand along her cheek, and then murmured, "Open your eyes, Amanda. I want you to look at me." She heard him shift and then she did as he had asked, and found herself looking into his deep, shining, liquid eyes. His hands found their way to her shoulders and gently held her against the cushions. "Amanda, we'll find a way," he said softly. "You'll keep discovering new problems until you're ready, Mandy, but I'm telling you — and asking you to believe — that the problems aren't serious; they're not insurmountable," he murmured, his lips a breath away from her own. "All that's insurmountable is my desire for you, and the truth — that we're meant to be together." He inhaled deeply. "And I'll show you," he whispered, his breath warm against her cheek.

Slowly he lowered his mouth to hers, his warm lips covering hers and then gently parting them. His tongue flicked in her mouth, searching and exploring, gently and then thrusting, and he groaned and eased her back along the couch, moving his strong body on top of hers. Her hands moved along his back — the strong, muscled back she had wanted to hold for so long — and then found their way to the thick masses of hair at the nape of his neck.

He drew his head back and looked at her with heavy-lidded dark eyes. "I've wanted you so much, Amanda," he whispered huskily, his voice hoarse with desire. "God, how

I've wanted you." And he pressed against her then, and she felt the power of his desire with a flood of warmth that made her moan. "Oh, Eric," she cried, shifting her heated body against his.

He lowered his mouth to her neck then, marking a searing path to the throbbing pulse at her collar, down to the rise of her heaving breasts. He drew himself back, and Amanda looked at him through eyes half closed with passion as he rapidly unbuttoned her blouse with expert fingers. His hair hung down over his darkened face, and with a groan he lowered his head, and Amanda held him, her hands clutching at his hair as he flicked his tongue across a nipple, bringing it to a hardened tip of desire as he teased the other one with his fingertips. His mouth descended then and sucked gently, his tongue flicking at the hardened tip, and he closed his teeth around it and gently tugged, making Amanda cry out, her fingers tangled in his hair.

And then he raised his head and looked at her with cloudy eyes. "All right," he said hoarsely, "that's enough." And he raised himself off her, pushing his hair back from his face as he stood.

"I don't understand," she said quietly, still in a haze of yearning.

"You said you weren't ready, Amanda. I don't want any recriminations. I just want to give you a little taste of what you're missing," he said hoarsely. "What we're both missing." He turned to her then and looked at her tenderly. "I'm sorry if that sounds harsh, Amanda. It's just that pulling away from you like that is pretty harsh treatment in itself — it's not easy for me. At all."

"It wasn't easy for me, either," she answered, sitting up and buttoning her blouse. "Just because I might not be completely ready emotionally doesn't mean I don't respond to you, Eric." She smiled. "Obviously."

He smiled. "Obviously. But I'm serious, Amanda. Regret can destroy all kinds of things that are meant to live. Like a drought that kills a seedling before it has time to live and grow and bear fruit." He shook his head. "It's not something I want you to feel about us, ever."

Amanda nodded and smiled wistfully. "All right," she said.

And he kissed her gently on the lips.

When Amanda and Eric said good-bye to each other outside his apartment — he to go down to the DA's office, she to return to commission headquarters to interview

Sheila Farnham — they arranged to have dinner the next night, at Amanda's apartment.

"I'll be looking forward to it," Eric said, "and you call me if the information Sheila gives you isn't enough background for the profile, Mandy."

"I will," she agreed, and after a quick kiss they parted to go in opposite directions.

On her way back to Eric's office, Amanda thought of nothing but Eric and the searing embraces they had shared, of his lips parting hers and his strong body urging her on. Yet he had been the one to halt the encounter; he was the only one of them able to know her true feelings.

Yet now that she was alone, away from the impossible distraction of Eric's physical presence, she realized that in one sense Eric was wrong. For though she was haunted by years-old whisperings of guilt and fear, she loved him. It was that simple, and she smiled and then laughed at the thought; it was simple and lovely and clear. She loved him and wanted him. And though there were problems, who was to say they couldn't be worked out? What was important was that what she had been waiting for — for more than seven years, for her whole life — had happened. And Eric seemed to feel the same way, though he hadn't said it in so many words.

She frowned, wishing she hadn't let Eric stop, wishing she had made love with him as her body had so achingly urged her to do. But then she remembered something Eric had said back at his apartment — that regret was useless and destructive to hopes and wishes and relationships meant to live and thrive — and she determined to forget what was not even a true mistake, but perhaps only a misstep, and to look to the future. Eric was coming over the next night for dinner, and oh, would she be ready for him then.

Chapter Eight

When Amanda arrived at commission head-quarters, Sheila was quite friendly and said that Eric had called and asked her to give Amanda any information she wanted and that she was more than happy to help.

Amanda thanked her and called in to WKM to make sure no new stories had broken that she had to cover. Then she set up her tape recorder on Sheila's desk and began the interview.

"Sheila, what I'm going to do is just ask you a series of questions I think you're qualified to answer as Eric's press aide. After that I'll write up the introductory section of the close-up. If there's any question you feel uncomfortable about answering, please just let me know because I can ask Eric. Basically, we're just trying to save time, and Eric thinks highly enough of you to put the interview in your hands."

Sheila smiled, her brown eyes shining. "I won't have any trouble, Amanda. I'm intimately enough involved with every aspect of Eric's work to be able to answer any question you have."

Amanda nodded, a bit put off by Sheila's confidence. It had seemed clear this morning that Sheila was nothing more than a very young, very ardent fan of Eric's, the type of young woman to be found in all political campaigns and areas in which a man was a charismatic central figure. Yet Amanda wasn't entirely comfortable with the thought that Sheila spent virtually every working hour with Eric, as she herself had done seven years before. She knew the longings that could fire the heart in that context, knew the fantasies one could concoct.

"I'm so glad you're interviewing me," Sheila exclaimed, interrupting Amanda's thoughts. "It'll give me another chance to show Eric just how indispensable I am to him."

Amanda smiled frostily and turned on her tape recorder.

"After all," Sheila continued, "when he wins the nomination, he's certainly going to need someone like me to deal with the press — not people like you, of course, but you know, the hostile ones." She smiled brightly. "And this morning he told me I'd probably be it!"

"It?" Amanda repeated drily.

"Sure," Sheila said happily. "I'm not sure

exactly what you call it — I guess press aide again, but maybe something higher. Anyway, I'll probably keep this job after the commission winds up and help Eric with the political campaign."

"But the commission might not wind up for months," Amanda stated, wishing her voice sounded more firm and less fearful.

"Oh, I wouldn't worry about that," Sheila said confidently with a wave of dismissal. "Eric told me it should wind down much sooner than that — within a couple of weeks probably. And then he'll be free to start the campaign in plenty of time for next fall — a year is more than enough time."

"I see," Amanda said flatly. "So in your opinion the nomination is virtually definite."

Sheila shrugged in a manner disturbingly reminiscent of Eric; as if she had been with him so much lately — and she had, in fact — that she had unconsciously assumed his mannerisms. "Well," Sheila said slowly, "as far as I'm concerned, Eric should be packing for Washington right now."

Amanda frowned. "I doubt that's your official statement, Sheila. I'm asking you in your capacity as Eric's press aide — not as his —" She hesitated; she couldn't quite say "admirer" or "fan." "As his friend," she finally finished.

"Oh," Sheila exclaimed. "Well, the official position is that Eric is undecided." She smiled. "But you *could* say that 'sources close to Mr. Harrison expect him to announce publicly his interest in the nomination,' or something along that line. That would be nice, and couldn't hurt a bit."

Amanda stiffened. "Miss Farnham," she began slowly, "I think we — or you, rather — are operating under a bit of a misconception. I'm not here as part of some sort of free publicity campaign. I'm here to research a report I am writing on Eric."

"I know," Sheila said calmly, "but you two were friends years ago. Eric himself said your close-up would do wonders for the campaign, and he wouldn't have said it if he thought you were against him in some way."

Amanda stared at Sheila. She certainly sounded sure of two things: that Eric planned to accept a nomination that would be forthcoming any day now, and that Eric was confident that Amanda's coverage of him would be very favorable. Both ideas depressed Amanda enormously, and she felt suddenly exhausted, tired of listening to Sheila and her adoring praises of Eric, tired of thinking about Eric and his damn career.

She asked the rest of her planned questions in a desultory manner, letting her tape recorder listen for her as her thoughts went elsewhere. Finally, feeling enough was enough, she turned off the recorder and looked at Sheila. "Okay, Sheila, I don't think I need any more information from you now. The profile will mostly consist of taped segments with Eric, anyway, so I have all the background information I need. Let's just set up a time for the taping."

Sheila frowned. "Well, all right," she said reluctantly. "But Eric said you'd be talking to me all afternoon. Shouldn't we discuss a few more things?"

"*I'm* writing the profile, Sheila. Not Eric. Just give me a time, please."

"Well, it'll have to be next week," Sheila said. "Eric's calendar's booked up for tomorrow and the next day, and then he's going to Washington for —"

"To Washington?" Amanda interrupted.

Sheila smiled and nodded. "Uh-huh. A part of the pre-campaign planning."

"I see," Amanda said quietly.

"How about next Monday, ten o'clock. Film crew and everything?"

"Right," Amanda said distractedly, and a few minutes later was on her way back to the office, wondering how her problems with

Eric would ever be resolved. For he had clearly made extensive plans for the campaign, and obviously conveyed his enthusiasm to at least one member of his staff. And thus, though he had perhaps been truthful this afternoon when he had told Amanda that being with her was more important than anything, Amanda saw now that he had uttered his words in the heat of the moment — without meaning to be dishonest, but surely distorting the sad truth.

It was suddenly as clear as day that Eric would never voluntarily give up his political career — especially for a woman, when his first marriage had been so unhappy. Eric had *always* been ambitious; Amanda could recall hundreds of images — of Eric working all night at the office, of Eric bringing in more clients than any of the other senior partners at the firm, of Eric working, working, working. And he obviously responded to the sort of public adulation that Sheila was already a perfect example of. And there was nothing wrong with any of this, these needs, these ambitions. Except that they would all keep her and Eric apart.

Once back at the office, Amanda walked past Stan's office — he was on the phone as usual — but he glared at her and motioned for her to come in. She drifted in and settled in to the chair, not even listening to Stan's end of the conversation. What was the point when her relationship with Eric was destined to end before it had had a chance to grow? What was the point of anything?

The sound of Stan's slamming down the phone cut through Amanda's thoughts and brought her back to the present. He buzzed the intercom, grabbed the receiver, yelled "Get Al and the crew ready to leave in five minutes," slammed down the phone, and looked at Amanda. "You're going down to another press conference. Is that all you have to wear? Never mind. Be ready in two minutes. City Hall — the Harrison Commission. Guy named Greg Warner is going state's evidence, and the commission's blowing the city sky high. See if the morgue's got anything on this Warner before you go."

"I don't have to," Amanda said quietly, feeling as if she were speaking in a dream.

Stan raised his brows. "What — you mean you've looked? What?"

Amanda took a deep breath. "I used to be married to him, Stan," she said tiredly. "He's my ex-husband."

"Your what?" Stan exploded.

"My ex —"

"I heard you!" Stan yelled, his face reddening. He let out a stream of curses, shook his head, and glared at Amanda. "You're off the story," he said flatly, and picked up the phone again. He buzzed his assistant. "Get Jacobs in here. Yeah. Brief him on the Harrison stuff and then send him in. Right." He looked back at Amanda. "All right, look. I don't have time to discuss it now, Amanda." He looked at his watch. "Come back after the broadcast. In the meantime pick up Jacobs's research on that jail-overcrowding story. Get it from his assistant and get started, and I'll talk to you later."

As she walked through the maze of desks to Jacobs's assistant, Amanda wondered whether she had even said anything to Stan after he had told her to go; she could hardly remember where she was, much less what she had just said. All she could think about was Stan's anger, and the fact that she had just been kicked off her first two assignments at WKM. She didn't even know whether she was about to be fired or not. It wasn't entirely unlikely, she knew, as she imagined in painful detail what Stan was probably thinking at that very moment: that she had been trouble from the beginning, that she was exactly the kind of reporter the station didn't need at this crucial time in its development. And he would also wonder if she had known of Greg's guilt, and withheld this knowledge from him and from the viewing public as well.

Amanda was so vague with Jacobs's assistant that the young man had to ask several questions to determine what Amanda wanted. And when she headed back to her office with the files, she bumped into two desks before arriving at the little glass-enclosed cubicle she suddenly considered an island of safety.

Automatically, she opened the folder and began to try to read. But the words swam before her eyes, and she knew it was useless even to try to work at that moment. And then she realized she could call Eric; perhaps he hadn't left for the press conference yet, and his strong, comforting voice was certain to make her feel better.

But an unfamiliar voice said Eric had already left, and Amanda hung up without bothering to leave a message. Somehow she managed to pass the time, and finally, just before it was time for the broadcast, Vivian came in, her usual smiling self. But when she saw Amanda's expression, her smile faded. "Hey, Amanda, what's wrong?"

Amanda explained the little she knew — she still had no idea what Stan had in mind for her — and then tried to smile. "Well, at least it solves my problem with Eric. If I'm out of a job, we won't have to worry about *that* conflict of interest." She shook her head. "But it's certainly the worst solution *I've* ever heard, Vivian. I want to work, not end up being in a relationship by default."

Vivian waved a hand in confident dismissal. "Relax, Amanda. Stan's not going to fire you. It's not your fault your ex-husband is a crook." She smiled apologetically. "Sorry. But you know what I mean. Anyway, Stan will just keep you off the story, which makes good sense."

Amanda sighed. "I hope you're right. I just wish I could speak with Eric. I wish I knew how it had all happened."

Vivian looked at her steadily. "Do you blame Eric for what happened?"

Amanda shook her head. "No, I really don't. I blamed him before, for the investigation. Not that I thought placing blame on him was logical, but it was where my heart led me. Especially with the complications and jealousies of seven years ago underlying my feelings." She sighed. "But now that something has actually happened, and Greg has confessed, somehow I feel *less* upset over Eric's role than before. I might have been involved in the coverage, too, yet I'm not 'out to get' Greg, so there's no reason to assume

Eric is out to get him either." She sighed and shook her head. "I just hope . . . I just hope it's not too serious, and that Greg hasn't done anything really terrible."

Vivian shrugged. "You'll know soon enough. The news is coming on in five minutes."

"Oh, no," Amanda said quietly, dreading what she was about to see.

The story was practically a lead report — third from the top — and Amanda nearly fainted when the familiar City Hall press room appeared on the screen. Amanda stood quietly at the edge of the group watching the show, and girded herself for the report.

Jacobs, her substitute, stood at the back of the press room, microphone in hand, and looked into the camera. "This afternoon, the Harrison Commission's investigation into corruption in city-licensing practices achieved a major breakthrough following the confessions of Gregory Warner, a prominent real-estate broker in Manhattan. Warner, confessing to over fifty counts of bribery of public officials, has been promised a 'certain degree of immunity' according to DA Arthur Greenfield, in return for supplying the commission with extensive evidence allegedly linking several public officials to apparently massive corruption. We switch now to Eric Harrison, chief counsel of the commission."

The camera shifted and moved in for a head-and-shoulders shot of Eric. Amanda's heart skipped a beat. Eric looked extremely tense, the beads of sweat at his temples and the jagged line of his jaw betraying his feelings. His lips were set grimly, and his brows were drawn together in anger and tension.

Amanda's heart went out to him as she watched him hesitate, looking out at the reporters, scanning their faces, his eyes roving from left to right and back again. He looked pained, a far cry from the usual picture of a man whose team has achieved its goal. He looked desolate, as if he hardly wanted to bother with the conference at all. And then, as his eyes scanned the group of reporters one more time, Amanda realized all at once that he was looking for her.

She wanted to run to him then, tell him that she loved him and didn't blame him for what had happened. She knew, as she looked at Eric's searching liquid eyes, at the handsome face darkened with shadows of fatigue, that Eric doubted her feelings, now more than ever.

Eric cleared his throat and then began to

speak, clearing his throat once more. "We have . . . taken a major step, with the help of Mr. Gregory Warner, who is as of this afternoon cooperating fully with the office of District Attorney Greenfield. Several indictments will follow shortly." He paused. "That's all I have to say at the moment, but I will entertain questions from the press." He nodded. "Yes?"

"Is this Warner receiving protection?"

"Uh, that matter is under discussion at the moment." He looked into the WKM camera then, and Amanda inhaled sharply; it was as if he were looking right at her, as if, knowing she was watching, he wanted to look into her eyes and say he was sorry.

"What about the others?" a reporter yelled. "Can't you give us some names, Harrison?"

Amanda eased herself off the desk and quietly left the room. She didn't want to hear any more abrasive questions yelled out by reporters who were totally indifferent to the pain felt by Eric . . . and, somewhere, Greg . . . and Amanda. Amanda hated the fact that usually she herself was seen as a callous reporter oblivious to the sufferings of all those connected with a story. But for now what bothered her was the sadness of the whole situation. Greg had finally gotten himself into troubles he couldn't get out of, at least not easily; and Eric was obviously disturbed by what was a sullied victory at best. For though there could be no question about the justice of his mission — he would soon be responsible for having stopped an enormously dangerous network of corruption — Amanda knew that Eric was not pleased to have found Greg guilty. For aside from Amanda's part in the whole issue, Greg was, after all, an old friend of Eric's. Amanda knew that Eric was not without feeling or regret about having to achieve his own glory at the cost of an old friend's demise.

Alone in the ladies' room, Amanda leaned over the sink and rinsed her face with cool water. When she stood up and began to dry herself with a paper towel, she felt the beginnings of a headache nagging at the back of her neck, and she closed her eyes and softly swore.

She sat down, waiting long enough to be sure that the commission segment of the broadcast was over, and then went back into the newsroom to join the group. For while she wanted nothing more than to go home and lie down in the darkness to sort out her thoughts, she knew it was important to put on a strong front for Stan. He probably thought ill enough of her already without her adding weakness to the list of her problems.

When the broadcast was over, Stan guided her into his office, sat her down, and spoke. "I'm not going to ask what you knew, Amanda, because Harrison called me this afternoon and explained a good deal to me." He raised a brow. "I would have *liked* to hear it from you, but I know that would have been impossible." He sighed. "It's not a good beginning, Amanda, but it's just bad luck on your part, and I'm letting it pass. But you're off the story permanently. And we're canceling the profile on Harrison."

"Why?"

Stan shook his head. "He's too close to the damn nomination. If he accepts before the videotape is edited, which looks pretty likely to me, then we'll have to have every Tom, Dick, and Harry running for the Senate on the show because of equal-time regulations."

Amanda nodded absently. She was already thinking of something else. "You said I was off the story, Stan. But I'm not off politics, am I?"

"Of course not. Stay on Jacobs's old story for now." He looked at his watch. "And I suggest you go home and get some rest,

Amanda. You look like hell."

She laughed and was out the door, enormously relieved that Stan hadn't overreacted as many bosses would have, by switching her coverage to a nonpolitical area or, worse yet, by firing her.

Half an hour later, back at her apartment, Amanda undressed, put on a robe and slippers, ran a bath, and went into the living room to call Eric.

He answered the phone himself on the first ring, and Amanda was taken off guard, having expected to have to speak with Sheila first. "Uh, Eric."

"Amanda," he said breathlessly. "What happened to you? Where were you this afternoon? Are you all right?"

She smiled. "Yes, I'm fine, Eric. It's . . . it was a shock, I guess, to have it happen so soon. But if it had to happen, I'm glad it was sooner rather than later."

"I'm so sorry I didn't get a chance to tell you myself," he said, his voice caressing and caring. "I only found out after I left you and went down to the DA's office."

"I know," Amanda said quietly. "It's really all right."

Eric sighed. "I'm glad to hear you say that, Amanda, but we have a lot to talk about anyway."

Amanda smiled. "Why don't you come over, Eric? We don't have to wait for tomorrow night."

Eric sighed. "Actually, Mandy, about tomorrow night . . . there's been a change in plans. I have to fly down to Washington tonight. For a week, and —"

"A week? Eric, why? I thought you weren't going until the day after tomorrow."

"The schedule's changed," he said sadly. "And I'm more sorry than you can imagine. I wanted to be with you tomorrow night. Very much."

"Oh, Eric. I wish you didn't have to go."

He sighed. "So do I. But it's for the campaign. Several of the really important party members down in Washington want to meet with me, and they lined up all the meetings from tomorrow on." She could hear him sigh again. "It's not that I've forgotten our discussion . . . I'm trying to work things out, make a decision."

"About the nomination, you mean?"

"Yes. It looks more definite now than it did — well, than it did before tonight, frankly. But we can work things out, Mandy. I promise." He paused. "By the way, I hope that things are all right at your job. I spoke with Stan, but why weren't you at the conference?"

"Well, he took me off the story, but everything's okay." She paused. "I'm sorry you're going away, though. I had wanted to tell you . . ." her voice trailed off.

"Yes?" he said softly.

Amanda closed her eyes. Suddenly, she didn't want to tell him that her feelings had changed — that she no longer felt guilty, that she was ready to be together, to set aside her worries and guilts and fears. Speaking those words over the telephone — when Eric was canceling their dinner and about to leave town for a week — wasn't at all what she had had in mind. She knew that if she spoke up now, she would wish later on that she had waited and done it differently. For she wanted to be able to see the light in his eyes when she told him she was ready — the light of love as well as of desire — and feel his arms around her as she told him, feel his warm breath against her cheek, his lips near her own. No, she wouldn't tell him now. She wanted to see him when she did, and she would keep silent for the moment.

"Never mind," she said quietly. "But keep me up to date on all the Washington goings-on," she said briskly.

"You bet," he said, his voice low and affectionate. "I'll call you when I'm down there, Mandy, and I'll see you when I get back."

"Okay, good-bye," she said quietly.

"Good-bye, Mandy, I . . ." his voice trailed off. "I'll miss you," he finally finished, and paused again. "And I love you, Mandy. . . . Good-bye."

"Good-bye," she said quietly, wishing she had the courage to tell him she loved him. But something was stopping her as surely as if she had had a hand clapped over her mouth; and she replaced the receiver and only then, very quietly, said, "I love you, Eric. I do." Then she closed her eyes and smiled, recalling over and over how Eric had said those last words. *I love you, Mandy. I love you, Mandy.* She wished she had been able to answer him, to tell him that she loved him, too. And she would have, she knew, had he been with her instead of on his way to Washington.

And then she realized that underlying her happiness, there was anger — anger at Eric for leaving at this crucial time. For although she knew his meetings were important, and knew, too, that she would cancel a simple dinner date if she had an important assignment, she wished — irrationally — that he had found a way to juggle both sets of plans. Of course, he had no way of knowing that she had planned the evening to be a watershed of sorts, the beginning of a new and wonderful phase of their relationship.

She was angry with herself, too, for she wondered whether it was right for her to hope that Eric would forgo his political career for the sake of the relationship. Eric obviously loved the political arena; when he spoke about his plans, his face lit up with an enthusiasm Amanda loved. And she was, in effect, telling him that he would have to make a choice between her and his career. Was that fair? Was it right?

And she wondered, too, what she would do if Eric turned around and made similar demands on her. Would she be able to turn her back on political coverage, something she had worked toward for six years? Would she even want to try? Making a decision to give it up would be tantamount to giving up her entire broadcasting career; finding another job in television in New York — or anywhere — was virtually impossible, and WKM had no use for anyone in any other area.

And then Amanda remembered something Eric had said recently, when Amanda had been feeling guilty about Greg and wondering whether she could have prevented some of his problems by staying married to him. And Eric had said that yes, perhaps she would have prevented some problems, and she would have also been throwing away her life.

If Eric decided to say yes to his nearly-certain nomination, and if he wanted to be as seriously involved with Amanda as he seemed to now, would she be able to turn her back on her career? Would she be able to play a role she had never even tried, as girl friend — or wife — of a Senate candidate?

She shivered at the thought, as she recalled a whole string of politicians' wives — clinging to their husbands, a frozen smile on their faces every time a camera flashed, speaking to the press very carefully, very quietly, as they had no doubt been briefed to do by their husbands' staffs. There were exceptions, of course, but the mold was the same in the greater percentage of cases. It was a life of limits — limited exposure to the public, limited points of view, limited time with one's husband. And Amanda knew then that she would only be able to perform that role if and when it were *her* choice — under no pressure to do so — and if that time ever came, it would surely be a few years away, after Amanda had sufficiently established herself in her career.

And that meant it was now up to Eric. He had just told her he loved her. Now the question was how much that meant to him, and if he wanted Amanda enough to forsake his dreams.

Chapter Nine

The week in which Eric was away passed quickly for Amanda. She was on the air daily, having taken over Alan Jacobs's series of reports on prison overcrowding. The preparation of the broadcasts took up almost all of her time, and by the end of each day she was exhausted but happy, relieved that she had completely redeemed herself in Stan's eyes, and had received some outside recognition in the newspapers as well, when her name was mentioned as the papers picked up her story and amplified it in print. This was work at its best, and Amanda loved it.

Eric called her almost every evening, and they had pleasant but muted conversations, full of tacit questions that remained unanswered, quiet words of affection brimming with unexpressed hopes. It looked, indeed, as if Eric would receive the nomination for the primary, if he wanted it. And that was the way he expressed it in each conversation, emphasizing that it was his *if he would accept it.*

Amanda couldn't bring herself to confront Eric with her feelings, her questions, her hopes. She rationalized her silence by telling herself that it was too early to force an actual confrontation, that she had hardly embarked on the new phase of the relationship. But she suspected that the real reason for her silence was far less rational, far less reasonable: She was afraid to hear him say no. No, he couldn't possibly give up his political plans; no, he had no plans to commit himself to Amanda; no, there was no reason for either one of them to give up a career, because their relationship wouldn't last.

And so, whenever she spoke with Eric, she let the silence grow between them — as he did — and they spoke only of the present — of his meetings in Washington, of her broadcasts in New York. And when each conversation began to come to a close, and the silences grew heavier, Amanda hoped he would tell her he loved her again. But he didn't. And she grew more achingly aware of her reticence of the other night, when he had told her he loved her and all she had said was good-bye. She told herself that was why Eric no longer said it. He wanted to hear those words from her, as well. At least she hoped that this was so.

The night before Eric was due to come back, he called Amanda and told her when he was due in, that he'd have to work on some commission business with the DA that afternoon and then wanted to see her. She invited him to her house for a late dinner — she wouldn't be able to leave the newsroom until eight — and they said good-bye.

Amanda found a supermarket open late that night, and stayed up quite late, preparing as much as she could in advance. She marinated the chicken in a delicious mixture of red wine, soy sauce, brown sugar, and ginger, cleaned up the living room and the kitchen, stuffed as much of her bedroom clutter into one of her closets as she could, and finally fell into an exhausted slumber at three A.M.

She was awakened in the middle of the night — at four thirty, she discovered when she turned on her bedside lamp — by the ringing of her phone. She answered with the panic she always felt when her phone rang at this time of night.

"Hello?" she answered warily.

" 'Manda," a voice slurred. "How're you doin'?"

"Greg," Amanda breathed. "Where have you been? I've tried to call you a dozen times."

"You and that Harrison. I heard about you two."

Amanda sighed. "Greg, where are you?"

"Out," he said childishly. "Out and you don't care."

Amanda closed her eyes. "I do care, Greg. And I care about what happened to you."

"Yeah, sure," he sulked. "Sure you care." He coughed against the receiver, and Amanda heard a horn blare in the background.

"Are you — it'll all work out, you know," she said. "I know it will."

"Oh, yeah, sure. Sure. You have Harrison arrange it, and that'll be just great." There was a clatter, and Amanda heard "Bye" from a distance, and then a click as Greg hung up.

She sighed and replaced the receiver and turned out the light. She felt sorry for Greg — for all he had done, for all he would probably continue to do in the future if given the chance.

And she was grateful to him, too, for something she had just learned: He *did* still blame her — for all that had gone wrong in his life since the divorce. And none of it was her fault. But it showed her how wrong it was to be dependent, to ask too much of another person. She had no more right to ask Eric to forgo his political plans than Greg had had the right to expect her to stay married to him against her will. Eric would have to make his own decision — with no pressure from her — for the relationship ever to work. For if she pressured him, even subtly, and he acquiesced in her wishes, wouldn't he resent her for as long as he still wished to pursue his plans, if not forever?

Amanda soon fell asleep and awakened the next morning, despite her short sleep, early enough to add a few more welcoming touches to her apartment. She still felt a certain elation over her decision of the night before that she would allow Eric to make his own decision, and then live with whatever fate had dealt out. It was a mature decision, she felt, and one that could allow her to be with Eric without constantly questioning his directions and motives.

The day flew by, and soon Amanda was home, getting ready with an hour still left before Eric was due. Her apartment looked better than ever. With sprays of autumn leaves set in tall vases round the living room, and candles lit here and there, Amanda had created a cozy, welcoming atmosphere. And the baking chicken had filled all three rooms with a delicious gingery aroma.

Amanda put on a beige silk at-home set that fit rather well since she had lost weight, the top just catching against her breasts and the pants fitting smoothly over her hips and then hanging gracefully down to her ankles. The pinkish-beige color went well, too, with her auburn hair and blue eyes. But she was a bit nervous about wearing the outfit, for the young woman she saw looking back at her from the mirror was a woman clearly on the path of seduction, her breasts pulling against the blouse when she moved, and the whole outfit suggesting it could be removed — or torn off — in a second. But she *did* want to look attractive, so she finally convinced herself not to change.

Some time later the doorbell rang, and Amanda ran to the door, still lightened by the elation she felt over her previous night's decision.

And when she opened the door, she matched Eric's broad smile as his eyes roved appreciatively over her face and figure. He looked better than she had ever seen him, his dark eyes shining, his broad shoulders and chest handsomely filling his white cotton shirt, his hair dark and lush.

"You look beautiful," he said silkily, his voice low and eyes flashing. He leaned forward and kissed her lightly on the mouth and stepped in, his arms full of packages. "Now," he said, laying them down on her foyer's end table. "Here," he began, handing her a florist's bouquet, "is something I wait for every year."

She looked inside and smiled. They were winter berries, beautiful, heavily laden branches thick with red berries that would go perfectly with all the foliage around the room. "We obviously have the same taste," she observed with a smile, gesturing behind her at the fall leaves.

"Of course we do," Eric agreed, grinning. "And here, darling, is a torn relic, a symbol for the two of us."

Amanda laughed. It was the campaign poster that Hal Jenkins had designed for Eric, with the words, "Sorry, not for now — I have better things to do," written across the center.

"And here's red, and white," Eric said, holding up a bottle of wine in each hand, "since I didn't know what we were having."

Amanda smiled. "Great," she said, taking both bottles from him. "Come on into the kitchen and we can open the red. Even though we're having chicken, it's been marinating in red, so this will be perfect."

As Amanda set the water for rice on the heat and mixed the salad dressing, Eric opened the wine and poured. It was a nice repeat of the domestic scene at Eric's house, and Amanda loved it. That sort of domestic calm was something she hadn't experienced since the first few months of her marriage with Greg, and she had begun to doubt she ever would again. She was glad, too, that Eric wasn't a man afraid — out of some misguided paranoia about masculinity — to go into the kitchen and cook.

When Eric picked up the wineglasses to take them into the living room, he glanced at the flames under the rice and then at Amanda. "Let's not eat for a while yet," he said softly, and exchanged a heated look that sent a sudden rush of warmth through Amanda as she realized she'd probably be in Eric's arms soon. She turned off the flames and followed him into the living room, her eyes on his firmly muscled back, on his slow walk, which suggested pleasures that made her blood run hot, her lips parted in desire.

He kicked off his shoes and sat on the couch, and she followed suit, and then they raised their glasses in toast. Eric smiled, gazing into Amanda's eyes. "I don't give a damn in hell if this sounds corny, Amanda, because I mean it: To us — to a future together that we were meant to have, that's more important than any job, or career, or problem we may ever have to face."

"To us," Amanda answered softly, clinking her glass against Eric's.

And they drank, looking into each other's eyes, and Eric slowly smiled. "What's different?" he murmured, eyes roving over her face.

"What do you mean?" she asked softly, mesmerized by the nearness of him, by the pull of his dark, heavy-lidded eyes, the lips that could ignite her so easily, so fully. "What do you mean?" she repeated vaguely, softly, not remembering whether she had answered him, so hypnotized was she by his eyes.

Eric laughed. "This wine must be stronger than I thought." He looked at her curiously. "I came here with an announcement of sorts." He gestured toward the foyer. "That's what the campaign picture was all about — that I'm not running after all." Amanda's heart leaped. "But you seem different — you seemed glowing, happy, before I even told you — as if you had somehow known, or as if you had accepted the possibility of my running." He slowly shook his head. "All the worry, all the tension is gone from your face."

Amanda smiled and shrugged. "I made a decision last night, Eric. I don't want to pressure you; I have to let you make your own decisions freely, as you've let me make mine."

His eyes roved over her face, taking in her eyes, her lips, her hair. "But you *are* glad that I'm not running — ?"

She nodded. "Of course. Very. As long as it's your decision."

He smiled ironically and brushed a thick lock of hair back from his forehead. "Unfortunately," he said, "it wasn't really my decision at all. I wish I could say it had been." He shrugged. "After all the meetings, all the buildup, all the media garbage about me even *I* was beginning to believe, it looks as if they've decided to go with someone else. Thomas Greene, from Staten Island." Eric laughed. "And he'll probably win, too. I heard he just hired Hal Jenkins as his PR man."

Amanda reached out and covered Eric's hand with her own. "You're disappointed," she said quietly.

His eyes melted into hers. "Some, yes. Of course. But not that much . . . as much . . . if it means we can be together, Mandy."

She smiled. "Now I can safely tell you I think you'd make a great senator, Eric. One of the rare ones, one of the good ones. But you'll make a great lawyer, too, as you already are."

He reached out and his finger grazed down her cheek, along her lips, down her neck, and she closed her eyes, warm with desire for Eric's touch, aching to feel what she had felt of him before.

And then he lowered his mouth to hers, and she pulled him close, and her lips parted as Eric's tongue hungrily explored the warmth of her mouth and his hands wrapped around her waist. He drew his head back and looked into her eyes, his own eyes stormy with yearning. "I don't want to wait any longer," he murmured huskily.

She closed her eyes and sank her head back against the cushions. "Neither do I," she whispered, "neither do I." His lips descended on her neck, his wet mouth moving down from her ear to the beating hollow of her neck, to the rise of her breasts. She tangled her fingers in his hair and breathed deeply, the taste of him, the scent of him making her feverish with desire. And then he put one arm around her back and his other arm under the warming silk of her thighs and lifted her up off the couch. She wrapped her arms around his neck and trailed her lips along his throat as Eric carried her into the bedroom and laid her down on the bed.

He looked down at her with dark, blazing eyes and then lowered himself over her waist, a strong hard thigh to either side of her and his massive chest rising above her own. His eyes became soft and tender as he unbuttoned her blouse and pulled it off, exposing her already-hardened nipples.

She felt the strength and hardness of his rising desire and moved urgently under him, and as she raised her hips upward, he slid her pants down, his breathing coming faster as he took in her nearly-nude form. Then he eased off her and stood above her, his eyes focused on her one remaining garment, and he began unbuttoning his shirt, never taking his yearning eyes from her warm, waiting body.

"Wait," Amanda murmured, rising off the bed and standing before him. "Let me," she whispered. And standing in front of him she slowly unbuttoned his shirt and slid it down his arms and off. His shoulders and chest were magnificently muscled, covered with fine dark hairs, and Amanda grasped his firm, thick shoulders and leaned forward and sucked each nipple to a hardened point. Eric moaned and grasped at her, as she trailed her mouth lower, down the flat center of his stomach to his belt.

Slowly, tantalizingly, she undid his belt, unzipped his pants, and slid them down. His legs were beautifully muscled, strong and lean and dark, and her eyes roved over him, drinking in his masculine beauty.

She reached down and pulled Eric's one remaining bit of clothing off, and moaned and trailed her mouth down along his stomach, her tongue flicking and her teeth gently grazing until Eric cried out her name. He grasped her shoulders with burning hands and guided her back along the bed. He lowered his length on top of her, his every inch all muscle and desire, his mouth trailing a wet searing path from her neck to each nipple and down, as he slid along her heated skin to the line of her underpants. He pulled them off roughly, and then drew himself back and looked at her, his eyes hungrily roving over the length of her heated body.

"Is it finally right now? Do you want me, Amanda?" he whispered hotly in her ear.

"Yes," she moaned hoarsely, writhing underneath him, wanting to feel every inch of him.

He ran a warm hand down along her body and began slowly massaging her inner thigh, moving upward, slowly upward, as Amanda writhed more hungrily underneath him.

"How can we be sure?" he breathed, and then nipped at her lobe, sending a hot wave of desire coursing through her in undulating waves. "How can we be sure?" he repeated huskily.

"I want you," she moaned, running her hands along his back, scratching, coaxing him. "Take me, Eric."

His hand coaxed up along her inner thigh, sending rolling waves of passion through Amanda, making her mad with desire. "Take me," she groaned, at his taunting touch.

His lips closed over hers then, and he thrust his tongue into her mouth, and he breathed hotly into her ear. "Amanda, I want you more than any woman I've ever known," he moaned, his lean thighs burning against her own and then parting them forcefully. "I love you. I love you."

And as he claimed her lips with his, he made them one in a fiery thrust that made Amanda cry out, raking his muscled back and writhing with blazing pleasure.

"I love you," he breathed against her mouth, and as his teeth gently bit at the sensitive tip of her earlobe, she gasped, "I love you, Eric," and their undulating rhythm quickened with an urgency born of years of waiting, heavy desire that cried out to be sated, and Amanda was caught up in a swelling spiral of fire, of white heat and pulsating passion, as she cried out with Eric in a rolling, coursing blaze of pleasure that consumed them both.

They lay together, wrapped in each other's arms, silent, gently hugging. Amanda rested her smooth cheek against Eric's wet, rough one, and she could feel him smile, and then he drew his head back and looked at her with eyes filled with love. "I love you," he murmured.

She smiled and closed her eyes. "And I love you."

And he laid his head down again, and they both drifted off into a delicious, light sleep, though each knew dreams could never be as lovely as what they had just experienced.

Some time later they shifted gently and opened their eyes.

"Amanda," he murmured, holding her close, his hands warm on her back. "My Amanda. I'm so glad." He smiled. "We should have done this so long ago. My God —"

"Shh," she murmured, stroking his hair. "No regrets. Remember?"

He propped himself up on an elbow and looked down into her sleepy eyes. "I'm going to have to be careful with you, I can see."

She raised an eyebrow in challenge. "Why is that?"

He cocked his head. "If you remember everything I say, I can get into trouble," he said, curving a leg over the rise of her hips and moving himself closer.

"For instance?" she breathed, feeling his warmth against her. She ran a hand along his back and held him close, tingling again with the desire he had reawakened by simply touching her.

"For instance," he murmured huskily, "when I say I want to make love, and then let dinner wait —" He paused.

"Yes," she whispered hoarsely as she rolled back and he moved on top of her. She ran her hands along his back from his shoulders down to the small of his back, trailing light scratches that made him shift and roll, his scratchy chest raking her breasts to hardened peaks.

"You may think once is enough," he said hoarsely.

"I don't," she whispered, laughing. She sighed, molding her pliant curves to his hard, lean body. "Obviously."

"You may think that because I was able to hold myself back all those times," he breathed, stroking her thighs in a hypnotic rhythm, his touch gentle but firm, "that I can touch you and pull myself back."

"Can you?" She laughed, her breathing quickening with his.

He covered her mouth with his own and

then raised his head. "Never again," he breathed. "I can never touch you again without having you completely," he whispered, and molding her to him, they were once again joined in a white-hot spiral of coursing pleasure.

Afterward they lay exhausted in each other's arms. Eric brushed a wet lock of Amanda's hair back from her forehead and smiled. "You know, something smelled awfully good back there in the kitchen, Mandy."

She rolled her eyes and smiled. "You men. Obsessed with food."

Eric widened his eyes in mock anger. "Just how many have you had in here?" he demanded.

Amanda laughed and raised an eyebrow. "And how about you? What about that little groupie in your office?"

"Sheila?" Eric smiled. "She just adores me, that's all." He shrugged, looking amusedly helpless. "I'm a sucker for admiration, Amanda. That's why I was going to go into politics."

Amanda inhaled deeply and held up her palms. "Let's stop right there." She smiled. "Now what were you saying about eating? I'm famished myself."

"Good. I hate eating alone."

Amanda stretched lazily and sat up as Eric settled back in the pillows with his arms behind his head. "I have an idea," she said. "I certainly don't feel like waiting around for water to boil for rice and all that, so why don't I just bring us some wine with the chicken and we can eat in here."

"Sounds wonderful," he murmured, pulling her forward for a light kiss. "My sentiments exactly."

And they spent the rest of the night eating and making love, sleeping and talking, guided only by their wishes and their bodies rather than by time or convention.

The next morning — a Saturday — Eric didn't have to go in to the office until the afternoon, and Amanda didn't have to go in at all. They spent the day walking in the park by the river, hand in hand, reveling in the joy of being together — without worry or fear, without thinking of the past, or future. They went to a delicacy store and bought all their favorite foods, choosing exactly what they wanted even though the combinations were unusual: Brie and salami, peasant bread and caviar, hand-pressed cider and rare red wine; and they picnicked once again at Amanda's apartment, alone together in a world that barred time and worry from its door.

When it was time for Eric to leave, he looked as unhappy as Amanda felt, and kissed her long and hard at the threshold.

"There's a dinner tonight," he said hesitantly. "I'm not sure it makes sense to go, but —"

Amanda frowned. "What kind of dinner?"

Eric shrugged. "A Democratic fund-raiser — for the nomination. Now that Thomas Greene's candidacy is virtually in the bag, it seems silly to go. But it would look bad if I didn't — you know, sour grapes and all that." His dark eyes roved over her face. "I'd much rather spend the evening here, or at my place . . . in front of the fire." He sighed. "But I should go. And I'd like you to come, Amanda, if you would."

"Of course," she said. "And there's always later, Eric. We're not going to spend the night at the dinner."

"Oh, no," he said huskily, taking her in his arms and pressing her against his lean body, "I'm spending the night with *you,* woman." His dark eyes glowed like the banked embers of a fire. "I'll never have enough of that sweet ecstasy I see in your face, that fiery responsiveness . . ." He lowered his mouth to hers and parted her lips, moaning as he pressed her closer. She moaned in response, filled again with the burning need he had created in her, wanting to join with him in the blazing union of their desires once more.

Suddenly he thrust her away from him and shook his head, breathing heavily. "I've got to get out of here or I'll never leave," he said hoarsely. "I'll pick you up at six, Mandy. And it's pretty formal."

"Okay," she called as he walked down the hall. "I'll see you later."

Amanda spent the rest of the day as if in a wonderful dream, happier than she could remember ever having been. She felt fulfilled in a way she never had before, and she felt lucky — dangerously lucky, a dark inner voice tried to warn her — for she had the man she loved, and her career, and a future that looked as bright as a full moon on a summer's night.

Chapter Ten

As Amanda and Eric walked through the lobby of the Waldorf-Astoria, Amanda gently nudged Eric with her elbow and glared at him. "You didn't tell me the dinner was at the Waldorf, Eric," she complained jokingly, flashing her blue eyes at him. "And you call this 'pretty formal'? I feel like a rag picker!"

Eric laughed, throwing his dark head back and roaring deeply with pleasure. He looked at Amanda and shook his head. "You look beautiful, darling, and you would even if you *were* dressed in rags."

Amanda smiled, still in a state of half disbelief that this tall, handsome man — who was expert at everything he did, from directing an audience as a conductor does an orchestra, to winning over a jury, to making an omelet, to making love — this man loved her. She had shared her most intimate pleasures and responses with him as he had with her, had clutched at him, dissolved in ecstasy with him as she had with no other man.

She took his arm, and they walked

through the elegant lobby, glancing in at the restaurants and arcade shops, all done in different decors and color schemes.

Finally they came to the room in which the dinner was to be held and, after giving their names to a tuxedoed man at the entrance, were shown through beautiful gilt-edged double doors into one of the most lovely rooms Amanda had ever seen. Its high ceilings arched gracefully into a dome at the center of the room, with ornate gilt garlands edging the circle of the dome into graceful wedges that ended at the floor. There were hundreds of round tables covered with white linen tablecloths, with small bouquets of roses and tall, thin candles at each table. And almost everyone was in formal dress: the women in floor-length gowns, the men in black tie.

Amanda widened her eyes at Eric. "Can you believe this? Now I really feel like a rag picker!" she said.

"Forget it," he muttered, following one of the tuxedoed hosts to a round table near the center of the room. "Who's going to notice? There are too many people. And I don't give a damn about that sort of thing, anyway."

Amanda smiled and sat down, ready to enjoy the evening. Eric pointed out various people to her — dignitaries, political figures with whom she was unfamiliar as they operated primarily behind the scenes, raising funds and carefully shaping candidates in ways the public never heard about.

Amanda found it all fascinating, but she was glad that her exposure to this sort of gathering would be limited if not nonexistent in the future. For the men and women all seemed extremely formal, the men talking amongst themselves in little groups while the women hung on to their husbands' arms or talked amongst themselves in near whispers.

A handsome gray-haired man in white tie and tails approached the table, and Eric's face lit up as he stood to shake the man's hand. "Ah, Winston, good to see you. I'd like you to meet Amanda Ellis. Amanda, Winston Knowles."

Amanda and Knowles exchanged handshakes and brief smiles, and then Knowles turned back to Eric. "Eric, may I speak with you privately?" he asked quietly, his face etched with worry and concern.

Eric frowned. "Of course, Winston." And after saying a few words to Amanda, he disappeared with Winston Knowles into the crowd.

He was gone for what seemed like an eternity. Two other couples, both in their fifties or sixties, sat down at the table and introduced themselves to Amanda, and soon everyone in the room had been seated, yet Eric was still not back.

Amanda heard a stirring from the far end of the room, and then Eric and Knowles came forward, out of the only group of people still standing.

Amanda watched, proud once again as she watched Eric walk through the crowd. But when he seated himself at the table, his face was drawn, and his eyes looked wary and disquieted.

"What happened?" Amanda asked quietly.

Eric shook his head, his jaw clenched, and when his eyes met hers, for a moment they were filled with regret and then he looked away.

There was a murmur of voices, and then a hush, and then Winston Knowles walked to the podium at the head of the room to surprisingly wild applause, Amanda felt, considering the subdued behavior she had witnessed earlier.

Winston Knowles was smiling. "Ladies and gentlemen. Welcome once again to what we are once again pretending is not a fund-raising dinner." There was a ripple of polite laughter. "Now I'd like to begin by introducing a man whom we hope will be the next Democratic candidate for the Senate." He smiled. "And when I use the word 'hope,' that is supposed to bring to your minds a question. Namely, how can we bring this about? How can we make this a reality?" He folded his hands. "And we all know that fund-raising is the answer. This is the first of many dinners and events of which you're all aware, but in a sense this is the most important one of all, for tonight we'll all have a chance to meet this young man, and see exactly why it is that we *know*" — his voice became louder — "there will be a *Democrat* once again in the next Senate seat." Applause interrupted him, and Knowles hushed it with his hands. "So. Without further ado, Eric Harrison!"

Amanda paled. She looked at Eric, and he turned to her, his brown eyes filled with pain, and then looked away. Then he flashed a smile, stood up, and slowly walked down the center of the room to the podium, all eyes in the room focused on him as applause rang out.

Eric stepped behind the podium, adjusted the microphone, and smiled again, as the applause began to die down. And when he began speaking, thanking the audience for their support, his eyes sparkled with inspiration and enthusiasm and he gestured with assurance and force as he continued. He was in his element — playing the crowd like an expert musician — and Amanda saw that he was already winning them over — had won them over already.

Amanda stood up and walked out of the room.

She walked out through the gilt double doors, down the carpeted hallways, through the lobby, and out into the street, the night air suddenly hitting her like a splash of cold water. A doorman hailed a cab for her, and before she knew it, she was back at her apartment building, running up the stairs.

When she opened the door, she felt tears welling up as she looked around; suddenly everything reminded her of Eric — the winter-berry branches he had brought, the bottle of white wine untouched on the coffee table, the torn campaign poster lying on the foyer table.

Amanda took off her coat and put the water on for tea, and angrily shoved aside the dishes she and Eric had used for breakfast and lunch.

How had everything turned so rotten so quickly? And what, exactly, had happened? It was clear, she realized as she looked back on the events, that Eric had truly not known he was going to be selected as the group's candidate for the primary, if for no other reason than that he would have dressed more appropriately for the occasion, for once setting aside his stubbornly casual style for convention's sake. Amanda guessed that, at the last minute, no doubt, the other candidate — Thomas Greene — had backed out for some reason, and Winston Knowles and the others who ran such evenings knew they couldn't conduct a fund-raising dinner without a candidate. Eric had looked extremely upset after he had come back from speaking with Knowles; it was evident that he hadn't wanted it all to happen that way.

Yet, once he had stood up behind that podium, once he was in front of the audience he loved so well, he had reveled in it, as enthusiastically as if he had planned the night's events — because it meant that much to him.

Amanda wished she hadn't left. It had been almost cruel, for Eric had to have seen her go. And she could imagine his eyes — those eyes that had searched for her at the press conference, searched though she was never to come, searched as they were probably searching for her now.

What was obvious and sad and unhappily

true was what she had dreaded for some time now: She and Eric could never be together. For he loved politics — the excitement of applause, the thrill of an audience, the challenge of hard work — and Amanda didn't want to take him away from that, not ever. She had made a solemn vow to herself, and she had meant it. For asking Eric to forsake his plans would be tantamount to asking him to forsake his dreams. Yet she couldn't be at his side, either as girl friend or wife, and play the role those women had played at that formal affair, forsaking her own plans perhaps forever.

She thought about returning to the Waldorf — just to be by Eric's side, to try to undo her silly and irrational act of leaving. Yet perhaps that would just complicate matters.

She had to let him pursue his dream; she had to force him to see that he should not make a sacrifice he didn't truly want to make.

Perhaps the best plan was simply to wait and see what happened. Leaving the dinner had been selfish and immature and unreasonable; perhaps it was best, then, to let Eric react as any man would — with anger, probably, or at least annoyance. Maybe then he would decide that it was indeed time to follow his dream, and set aside everything but that one goal.

Amanda's head swam; there was no way out. What had she been thinking? How could she plot and plan Eric's next actions like so many chess moves? He was the man she loved. How could she try to fool herself into thinking she wanted him to follow his dream if that dream didn't include her?

She undressed for bed, not even bothering to wash the dishes or clear away the sad reminders that Eric had ever been there, and fell into a deep sleep.

When she awakened the next morning, she remembered the events of the evening with deep sadness. And she realized, as she glumly contemplated going about her usual Sunday morning routine of reading the *Times* and drinking coffee, that she had expected Eric to call. No matter what sort of reaction he had had, it would have been natural.

Amanda decided to call him. She didn't know what she was going to say, or what was going to come of it, but she could think of nothing else to do that could possibly change their plight.

Eric answered on the first ring.

"Eric?"

"Amanda —"

"I'm sorry about leaving so abruptly, Eric. It must have looked awful. Not only to you, but to the others, to your audience."

Eric laughed. "I don't give a damn how it looked to them." Amanda was flooded with happiness until Eric's next words. "But we've got problems, Mandy." She waited, silent, dreading. "I suppose you figured out what happened —"

"You mean with Winston Knowles?"

"Yes. Thomas Greene backed out at the last minute — no one's sure why, but Winston said something about Greene's wife not wanting him to do it." Eric paused, evidently aware of the parallel to their own situation. "They couldn't have no one, Mandy, and many of them had been much more strongly in favor of me than Greene. It had been a toss-up, and I ended up coming out on top after all."

Amanda swallowed. "I see," she said quietly, her throat closing over rising tears. "Then it's what you've always wanted," she said.

He was silent.

"Dammit, Eric," she said in a voice low with tension. "I'm all for it — absolutely. Go straight to the top." She paused. "I just wish you had been more honest . . . before. With yourself as well as with me. You *wanted* that nomination. Go out and get it then."

She heard him sigh. "Without you," he said quietly.

"Yes, without me," she heard herself say, tears beginning to roll down her cheeks. "And I'll go on my own way. Without you," she added softly.

"It's not what I wanted, what I had planned," he said quietly.

"It happened." She stated it softly. "That's all that matters." She tried to smile through her tears. "No regrets, remember?"

"Right," he murmured. "Good-bye, Mandy."

"Good-bye, Eric," she said quietly, and replaced the receiver carefully in its cradle.

Chapter Eleven

Amanda gradually slipped back into her life again, though the regret and anger and sadness she tried to fight were always there, always lurking and waiting under her rare moments of contentedness and calm. Her work was all-consuming, or nearly so. Throwing herself into it with passion, she handled plum assignments of the sort she hadn't expected to work on for years, and a segment she and Vivian had worked on — covering the court system — was nominated for an Emmy.

Stan looked at her searchingly from time to time, apparently wondering — or perhaps he knew — what had happened between her and Eric. Vivian urged her to go out and have some fun, and Amanda occasionally accompanied her for drinks after work. She went out a few times with men Vivian thought were "divine," but after the first date, Amanda always made it clear that she wasn't interested.

Weeks passed, as the autumn lapsed into the chill beginnings of winter. Leaves fell, the sky grew gray, the wind grew bitter, and Amanda's heart grew heavier as she wondered how — and why — it had all gone so wrong.

She had found the man she loved — had always loved, she realized, when she looked back on past times. Through forces beyond both of them she and he had been free — a miracle, she would have thought seven years before, yet true. He had loved her, and she him.

And now they were apart once again.

She looked at the reasons that had kept them apart, when Eric had so wanted to be together: Greg, whose story had faded from the news as he had from her life; Eric's political career, which had begun quietly, the campaigning not due to begin for some months yet; and her own career. And as Amanda looked back on her recent triumphs, the hours of long, hard work that had led to industry-wide recognition, she wondered why it had all seemed so important. For though successful, she was lonelier than she had ever been in her life. Work didn't begin to satisfy her emotional needs. And hadn't she planned on taking a break from her career to have children and raise a family, if she ever met the right man? She had met the man of her dreams, and forsaken one dream in pursuit of another. Yet with all her professional success, all the prosperity, all the recognition, she still came home to a lonely, empty apartment every evening and ate a solitary meal, alone in her self-enforced prison. For that's what it was, and she had erected the bars and locked herself in without anyone else's help.

Amanda didn't have to live with these thoughts very long to know what she had to do. She would call Eric and see if his feelings had changed, and if not, open herself up to whatever fate had to offer.

And then on the second Sunday in December, when Amanda awakened and realized with a pang of sorrow that it was seven years, exactly, since she had left her first job with Eric, the phone rang; and Amanda knew it was Eric, knew with the certainty that had been born in her the moment her eyes had first met his.

"Hello?"

"Amanda."

She closed her eyes and smiled. "Hello, Eric."

"I thought you, uh, might like to celebrate the anniversary of that most bleak of all days."

Amanda laughed. "I think I'd like that very much."

And as soon as Eric arrived at her door and took her in his arms, as soon as his lips claimed hers with love and passion, as soon as his dark, liquid eyes told her how much he still loved her — and had missed her — she knew that nothing could ever keep them apart.

When they gently ended their kiss, they both said, "I —," and then smiled, and Amanda said, "You first."

Eric guided her to the couch and took her hand. "I've been doing a lot of thinking," he said quietly, his eyes roving over her face. "I'm sure you have been, too."

She smiled wistfully. "Especially lately."

He reached out with his other hand and held her palm in both of his. "Amanda, I don't want success of any kind unless I have someone I love to share it with. It's all seemed so empty lately, so purposeless." He took a deep breath. "I'd like to give up the campaign, Mandy. I want to be with you — not just as a couple, as two people who have hectic lives, demanding jobs, twenty-four-hour-a-day worries." He shook his head. "I don't need that much challenge. I want a *life*, Mandy, A home life. Kids. A wife who loves me. And whom I love more than anything or anyone in the world. If you'll marry me, Mandy, I promise I'll make you happy."

"Oh, Eric," she cried, throwing her arms around his neck. "Yes," she whispered, and looked into his eyes. "Nothing is more important to me than you, than being happy. And having your love. I'd give up anything for that."

He put his arms around her. "You don't have to, Mandy. I know what kind of life I want, and I'm not ready for politics. Not yet." He shook his head. "I let you go because I thought I wanted that nomination more than anything in the world, more than you. . . . And I thought I knew what I was doing. . . . But I was wrong."

Amanda smiled and raised a brow. "No regrets, remember?"

"I remember," he said softly, "and I love you." And he took her in his arms, and they finally made up for all the waiting as slowly and fully and deeply as only their love could allow.

We hope you have enjoyed this Large Print book. Other Thorndike Press or Chivers Press Large Print books are available at your library or directly from the publishers.

For more information about current and upcoming titles, please call or write, without obligation, to:

Thorndike Press
295 Kennedy Memorial Drive
Waterville, ME 04901
Tel. (800) 223-1244

OR

Chivers Press Limited
Windsor Bridge Road
Bath BA2 3AX
England
Tel. (0225) 335336

All our Large Print titles are designed for easy reading, and all our books are made to last.